# Old European Fairy Tales

An imaginative selection of traditional tales drawn from the ancient countries of Europe: from the Land of the Midnight Sun to Sicily, from France to Hungary and Russia. They include one or two old favourites like *The Golden Goose* and *The Little Mermaid* as well as many delightful tales new to English readers like the story of *Sampo-Lapelill* from Lapland and *Ljungby Horn and Pipe* from Sweden.

# Old European Fairy Tales

Chosen and retold by
Irma Kaplan

Illustrated by James Hunt

FREDERICK MULLER

First published in Great Britain in 1969 by
Frederick Muller Limited
110 Fleet Street, London, E.C.4

Copyright © 1969 by Irma Kaplan

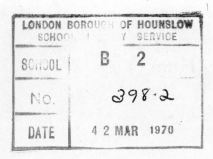
Printed and bound by Cox & Wyman Ltd London Fakenham
Reading
SBN 584-62385-2

# Contents

# Introduction

FEW STORIES, however skilfully told, have charmed and fascinated children or appealed to their fancy as much as traditional folk-stories, full of mystery and adventure. The oldest collection of this kind of stories was probably that of the frenchman Charles Perrault (1697). Later he had followers in almost every European country who told the same, or similar, stories with a few variations. The best-known of his followers are the brothers Grimm from Germany (1812-1814).

These stories have travelled from one country to another by word of mouth, and we may trace the plot of a story, or part of it, as far back as Greek mythology, the Old Testament, and from the Orient, too, through the collection of stories in the Arabian Nights. And even if only a few of these stories really originate from the country where it was first written, we may still call them French, German or Russian because each country has enriched them with creatures and beasts from folklore typical of their own, and given local names and customs to the places and people.

In this collection I have tried to avoid the internationally best-known stories of this type, but there are others equally fascinating and well worth remembering and being retold. I have chosen these stories not only because they are in some way typical of their own country, but also for their strange and exciting adventures, full of magic or humour, and most of all because they have been loved by all children of many generations.

These stories have all been retold for the children of today, except *Sampo-Lapelill* which is a translation from the famous Finnish author Zacharias Topelius (1818-1898). Apart from the exciting story, which contains a good deal of Nordic folklore, it gives an excellent description of the life of the Laplanders a hundred years ago, and of the winter in the Arctic Circle.

From another Nordic author famous all over the world, the Dane Hans Andersen (1805-1875), I have chosen the sweet story of *The Little Mermaid*. All of Andersen's tales are popular, so I chose this story that has been loved by readers in almost every language.

I felt that a collection of European fairy tales ought to include stories from Perrault and the brothers Grimm, so from the latter I have chosen *The Goose-Girl by the Well* which, perhaps, is less often told than the rest of their tales, but not less interesting. It was more difficult to find a story by Perrault which is not well-known to everybody, except stories which have little appeal for children of today. I have, however, told *Donkey-Skin* with a few considerable revisions.

The rest of the stories are all traditional, some with fairy creatures that are familiar in every country, and others with creatures typical of their country's folklore.

The three white-bearded old men in the story of *Marc the Rich and Vasilij the Unfortunate* are as well known in Russian stories as the trolls are in Nordic folklore. The trolls have been known in the Scandinavian countries from time immemorial. They were a reality to people in the early days of Christianity, and later people believed that until a child was christened it could not be safe from the spell of the trolls, as in *Sampo-Lappelill;* and that the sign of the cross rendered the trolls powerless, as in the story of *Ljungby Horn and Pipe.*

This story is based on a legend about an old silver drinking-horn and an ivory pipe, which, according to tradition, were stolen from the trolls, and are still kept at the manor house of the Trolle-Ljungby estate in the southern part of Sweden. The trolls were celebrating yule (Swedish *Jul),* which is the Scandinavian word for Christmas, but originates from the pagan celebration of the turn of the winter solstice which was supposed to be the trolls' festival. In the story of *Sampo-Lappelill* a similar celebration is related, but in Lapland it occurs later in the year.

# The Goose-Girl by the Well
*A story from Germany, based on the*
*original by the Brothers Grimm*

FAR AWAY ON THE MOORS at the foot of the mountains there
lived a very, very old woman. Her face was like a shrivelled
apple, her back was bent, and she limped about on a crutch.
She lived in a poor little cottage with her geese and every
morning she hobbled into the nearby forest to gather grass for
them and as much wild fruit as she could find for herself. Once
under the trees she was swifter and more vigorous than you
would imagine for someone as old as she seemed. When she
had gathered enough grass, she put it all in a huge basket which
she carried on her back, and she put the fruit she had found into
two big bundles, one for each hand. She should have collapsed
under such a burden, but somehow she always managed to
bring it all home safely. She seldom met anyone, but if she did,
she always greeted them with a friendly, "God bless you, dear
countryman! Fine weather today isn't it? You may wonder
why I'm toiling under this grass, but as you know everyone
has to carry his burden."

People were afraid of meeting her, and always went a long way round to avoid her if they could. Fathers pointed her out to their sons and whispered, "Beware of that old woman, my son, her ways are very strange, and she is certainly an old witch."

One morning a handsome young man came walking through the forest. The sun shone, the birds sang merrily and a gentle breeze rustled through the leaves so that he felt happy just to be alive. He could not have wished for a better start for his travels round the world to seek adventure.

He had not met a soul for hours when he caught sight of the old woman, who knelt on the ground cutting grass. She already had a large heap of grass and two big bundles with wild apples and hips by her side.

"Tell me, dear mother, how will you manage to bring all that home?" he asked.

"Alas, dear sir, I must carry my burden," she answered. "A rich man's child need not do it, but to the countryman we say,

> Bend your back, and work till late at night
> The ripening crop is your delight.
> The rich man has his pomp and power
> But few rewards at his last hour."

And while he stood beside her, pondering on her words, she continued:

"Perhaps you would like to help me? You still have a straight back and young legs so for you it would be an easy task, and my cottage isn't far away. It's just across the forest on the moor."

"I was only thinking on what you said. There may be some truth in what you say about the countryman, but you are surely wrong about the rich man? He, too, has hard work and much care even if it is of a different kind. I am the son of a rich nobleman, but I will show you it isn't only the farmers who can carry burdens. Would you let me carry your bundles?"

"Well, if you want to, I would be very grateful. It will take you at least an hour, but that will be nothing to you, will it? You must carry the apples and hips too."

The young man hesitated when he heard he had to walk for a whole hour, but the old woman took no notice. She lifted the basket onto his back, and gave him a bundle in either hand to carry.

"Look, how easily you manage it!" she said.

"Oh, no, not easily at all," answered the young man with a wry face. To tell the truth, the basket on his back was as heavy as if it were full of stones, and the apples and hips in the bundles felt like lead weights.

"Your things are really a bit too heavy. I can hardly breathe." He felt like putting all the bundles down and escaping as fast as he could but the old woman wouldn't let him do that.

"Can you believe it!" she said scornfully. "The young nobleman isn't capable of carrying things which I, an old woman, have been obliged to drag along for so many years. Rich people like you are quick to offer fine words but when it comes to the real thing they won't share the work.

"Don't stand there staring, get a move on! Don't think anyone else will come to your aid!"

As long as they kept walking on even ground he could just manage, but soon they went uphill and then it was almost more than he could stand. The stones slipped and rolled under his feet as if they were alive. The sweat poured down his face, and he burned hot and then shivered with the cold. His breath came in short gasps.

"No! This is too much for me!" he cried out, "I can go no further. I must have a rest."

"No, no, certainly not!" answered the old woman. "When we arrive home you may have a rest. But now you must go on. Who knows what good it may do you?"

"Old woman, you have gone too far!" cried the young gentleman. He tried to throw off the burden but he couldn't. The basket sat on his back as if it was glued there. He wriggled and turned but it made no difference. The old woman only laughed at him and hobbled about on her crutch.

"Don't get angry, dear sir," she said. "Your face is red as a rooster. Carry your burden with patience! When we get home, you will have your reward."

What could he do? He was forced to give in and trudge close upon the heels of the old woman. It seemed as if she was getting brisker and brisker while the burden was getting heavier and heavier.

Suddenly with a spring she leaped on top of the basket and settled herself comfortably between his shoulders. And though she looked like a bag of bones, she weighed more than the fattest matron. The knees of the young man trembled, but each time he stopped, the old witch beat his legs with a rod or with nettles.

Groaning and moaning, he climbed slowly up the slope, and finally they reached the witch's cottage. By this time he was on the point of collapse.

A long row of geese waddled towards the witch, stretching their long necks and flapping their wings crying, "raap, raap".

They were followed by a big, ugly woman with a rod in her hand.

"Mother, dear," she said to the old witch, "has anything happened to you? You are unusually late this morning, and I was rather worried."

"Oh, no, my dear Daughter," answered the woman, "nothing

bad has happened to me, quite the opposite, for this friendly young gentleman has carried my burden for me. And can you believe it, when I grew tired he carried me on his back as well? The way home didn't seem at all long, for we were joking and laughing happily the whole time."

At last the old witch jumped down from the top of the basket and lifted it off the young man's back. She took the two bundles he still carried in his hands, and then she looked at him kindly and said: "Please sit down on this bench outside the door, and have a good rest. Now you have earned your reward honestly, and you shall certainly receive it."

Then she turned to the goose-girl and said, "Go inside, my dear, it doesn't become you to stay here alone with a young gentleman. Don't add fuel to the flames for he could easily fall in love with you."

The young man didn't know whether to laugh or cry. "Such a little darling would be in no danger from me even if she were thirty years younger."

Meanwhile the old woman stroked her geese as if they were children and then went inside the cottage with her ugly daughter.

The young man stretched out on the bench. The air was mild and round the cottage lay green meadows dotted with cowslips, daisies and other gay wild flowers. A tiny, clear stream ran down from the mountains through the grass and the white geese waddled to and fro splashing in the water.

"It's really pretty here," he thought. "But I'm so tired I can hardly keep my eyes open. I must sleep for a while. I just hope a sudden breeze doesn't blow my legs off for they feel as brittle as straw."

He awoke later to find the old witch shaking him. "Get up!" she said. "I may have been a little hard on you, but it hasn't cost you your life. Now here is your reward. You don't need money, I suppose, so here is something else."

Then she thrust a little box into his hand. It was cut out from one single emerald.

"Take good care of it," she said. "It will bring you good luck one day."

The young man sprang up. He felt thoroughly refreshed and fit to continue his walk again. Thanking the old woman for her gift he set off without even throwing a backward glance after her "lovely" daughter. He could hear the geese quacking for a long way but soon he came to the huge forest, thick with high trees and with scarcely any paths to follow.

For three whole days he wandered about in the wilderness, but at last he found a path that led out onto a highway which he discovered led to the main city of this kingdom, and he decided to visit it.

The young man was the only son and heir of the powerful Count Cuno, but as he knew no-one in this country he went straight to the royal castle to announce himself to the King.

"He might perhaps think it strange that I travel about alone like this. But I shall explain that I prefer it this way because I can enjoy an adventure better if I am alone," he told himself.

His presence was announced and the young count entered the large hall and knelt before the throne where the King and Queen were seated. Then he took out the little emerald box and placed it at the feet of the Queen as a gift, as was customary when a man of high rank visited a royal court.

The Queen bid him rise and hand her the box. But as soon as she opened it she collapsed unconscious and lay as if dead.

The young Count was immediately seized by the royal guard, and tried desperately to convince them of his innocence, but the Queen, recovering herself, opened her eyes and called out to the guard to release him. Then she ordered everybody to leave the room as she wanted to talk to the Count privately.

When they were alone, she began to cry bitterly, and said, "How can I enjoy all this honour and glory that surround me here! Every morning I awake in sorrow and distress. Once I had three daughters, and the youngest one was so beautiful that everyone who looked at her marvelled. Her cheeks were like apple blossoms in spring, her hair glittered like the rays of the sun, and when she cried, no tears, but pearls fell from her eyes.

"She was fifteen years old when the King called all his three daughters before his throne. When the youngest came before him it was like the rising of the sun.

"And the King spoke to them and said, 'My dear daughters, I don't know when my last hour will come. Therefore I shall decide now what share of my kingdom each of you will receive. I know that you all love me, but the one who loves me most shall be given the best inheritance.'

"Each of the daughters said she loved their father most. 'Come,' said the King, 'you must explain to me exactly how much you love me so that I can understand what you mean.'

" 'I,' said the eldest, 'love you as much as all my gold and jewels together.'

" 'I,' said the second, 'love you as much as all my most beautiful dresses.'

" But the youngest one was silent.

" 'And you, my dearest child, how great is your love for me?' asked the King.

" 'I don't know,' she said quietly, 'for I can think of nothing to compare with my love for you.'

"But the King insisted she should think of something. At last she said, 'The most delicious food would taste of nothing to me without salt, so I love you as much as I love salt.'

"The King flew into a terrible passion when he heard this. 'If you really love me as much as you love salt then you shall be rewarded with salt!' he cried. Then he divided the kingdom between his two elder daughters but ordered a bag of salt to be strapped on the back of the youngest, and sent two of his servants to take her into the wild forest.

"We begged the King to spare her this, but his anger was not to be appeased. And how she wept with grief when she left us! Her path was filled with the pearls that rolled down her cheeks.

"But it wasn't long before the King began to regret how he treated the poor child. He sent people out in all directions to find her, but there wasn't the slightest trace. All the pearls were gone, and we didn't know if the wild beasts in the forest had torn her to pieces. When I think of this I feel quite desperate, and I try to comfort myself by hoping that she is still alive. She might have found shelter in a cave somewhere, or perhaps some merciful people have taken care of her. But imagine what a shock it was when I opened this little emerald box, for in it lies a pearl, exactly like those that came from my daughter's eyes as she wept. So you can understand how moved I was at the sight of it. So, please, you must tell me how you found the pearl."

The Queen finished her story, and the Count, moved with pity, told her how he had met the old woman in the forest, and how she had given him the box. "But there was something strange about her and she is certainly a witch. Of your daughter I have neither seen nor heard anything," he said.

The King and Queen decided to seek out the old witch as soon as possible for they thought that where the pearl had been, there they would learn something of their daughter.

It was settled that the next morning the young Count would

set out with the King and Queen to lead them to the old woman's cottage.

The royal court had to travel in state and it took them the whole day before they reached the heart of the forest. So it was decided that they should put up their tents to camp there for the night and continue again in the morning.

While everyone was sleeping in the camp, the young Count sat thinking of the Queen's sad story, and worrying if he would find the old woman's cottage again without difficulty. At last he got up and wandered out of the camp, anxiously looking for the path.

It was a clear, calm night with a full moon sending her beams through the leaves. He walked through the trees for a while until he thought he had found the right path. But as he wasn't quite sure he climbed a high tree and decided to sit there for the rest of the night, in case he lost his way.

Out on the moor beyond the forest the old woman sat spinning in her little cottage. It was dusk and only a log in the stove gave a faint light through the shadows.

Outside, she heard the geese cackling hoarsely as they came back from the meadows.

Her daughter came into the cottage then but the old woman merely thanked her by nodding slightly. The daughter sat down at the spinning wheel and began to twist the threads as quickly as a young girl. They sat quietly beside each other for a couple of hours without talking. The silence was shattered by a sudden noise: something scratched against the window. Two glittering eyes looked into the room. It was the old night-owl which gave its cry "Twoo, Twoo" three times. The old woman looked up for a moment, then she said:

"Now, it's time, my dear Daughter, for you to go out and attend to your own affairs."

The daughter rose from her seat and went out. She walked across the meadow into the trees till she came to a well where three old oaks grew. The moon had just risen round and bright over the mountains.

The daughter took off a mask of skin that she wore over her face, and took off also three wide, wrinkled skirts which she wore one on top of the other. Then she stooped over the well and began washing herself. When she had finished, she dipped the mask into the water. Then she spread it all over the grass so that it should dry in the moonlight.

But what had become of the ugly woman! When she took off the grey mask, golden hair gleamed forth like sunbeams in the moonlight, and flared and rippled round her slender body. Her eyes were as clear as the stars in the sky, and her cheeks were the soft pink of apple-blossom. But the beautiful girl was sad. She sat down on the edge of the well and wept bitterly.

She sat thus for quite a while, and would probably have stayed even longer, but she heard something rustle and crackle in a tree near by. She sprang to her feet like a shot from a bow. At that moment the moon was hidden by a cloud, and the young girl slipped into her former disguise and disappeared like a flame blown out by the wind.

Quivering like an aspen leaf she ran back home. The old woman stood in the door, and the girl tried to tell her what had happened. But the old witch only smiled and said, "I already know everything." They went together into the room, and the old woman put another log on the fire. She did not sit down at the spinning-wheel again, but fetched a broom and began cleaning and sweeping.

"All must be fresh and clean in here," she said to her daughter.

"But mother dear, at this time of the night?" said the girl,

"why do you begin so late? What on earth has happened?"

"Do you know what time it is?" asked the woman.

"It is not yet midnight, but it cannot be far from it," the girl answered.

"Do you not remember that tonight it is exactly three years since you came to me?"

The girl grew frightened and said, "Please, dear mother, don't throw me out, will you? Where shall I go? I have no friends and no home to go to. I've done everything you have told me and you have always seemed pleased with my work; don't send me away now."

But the witch would not say anything except to answer, "I cannot stay here myself any longer. Tomorrow when I move away everything in here must be clean and tidy. So you must not hinder me in my work. Do not fear for yourself, you will certainly have a roof over your head, and you will probably be satisfied with the payment I'll give you. Now, go to bed, it is very late."

"But why can't you tell me what is to happen?" asked the girl.

"Once again I tell you, do not disturb me in my work. Go to bed now and sleep well. Tomorrow morning you shall not put on your skin-mask and those three skirts you usually wear. Put on that silk dress you had when you came here, and stay in your chamber till I call you!"

High in his tree in the forest the Count had been sitting looking out in the moonlight deciding what direction they would continue their journey tomorrow. His head began to nod and he was nearly falling asleep when he caught sight of a figure walking through the trees. He recognised at once the same goose-girl he had seen at the witch's cottage.

"Oh, here she comes!" he said to himself. "Once I've found

one old hag, I shall certainly find the other."

But how astonished he was when she took off her skin and began to wash herself in the well. What a dainty, slender girl appeared from under the three wide skirts, and what glorious golden hair spilled out from under her grey wig. The whole vision was so radiant that he simply gazed spellbound.

He hardly dared to breath. But he stretched as far forward as he dared and peeped down between the twigs at the wonderful sight.

He must have leaned forward too far for suddenly the branch rustled and cracked. Instantly the girl slipped into her disguise and fled like a frightened deer. And as the moon just then hid behind a cloud he couldn't see in what direction she had disappeared.

The young man returned to the camp where the King and Queen had slept fitfully. Long before sunrise they set out on their journey and it was not yet noon when they came to the edge of the moor and saw the tiny cottage.

The Count did not dare to tell the King and Queen what he had witnessed that night, because he was uncertain himself if it was real or just a vision in his dreams. He merely spoke of the possibility that the old witch might know where she was. And that was enough to make the King and Queen shine with happiness.

The geese were crowded outside the little cottage, their cackling hoarser than ever. No goose-girl was to be seen, but when they peeped in through the window they saw the withered old woman sitting at her spinning-wheel, her head moving to and fro, but she didn't look round. The little cottage was clean and bright.

The King and Queen stood for a while looking in, not daring to enter, but at last they knocked quietly on the window. The old woman seemed to have expected them for she rose at once and said kindly, "Come in, I already know who you are."

And when they had filled the little room, she continued, "You could have saved yourself this long journey if you had not treated your daughter unjustly and cast her into the wild forest. No one could have wished for a more lovable and dutiful child. Fortunately no harm has come to her with me. She has been my goose-girl for these three years and has learned nothing evil from the geese. You, however, have spent the time punished by the fear and despair in which you have lived, and have learned a hard lesson."

She went to the little chamber where the Princess waited and called out, "Come in here, my dear little Daughter!"

Then the Princess appeared dressed in her silk dress with her golden hair shining round her pretty face, and her eyes glittering for joy as she caught sight of her father and mother.

She flung her arms round their necks and kissed them. And all of them hugged each other and wept for joy.

When she noticed the young man who stood near them she blushed like a rose, although she couldn't think why.

"My dear, dear child," the King said, "I have given away my noble kingdom. What have I now to give to you, my dearest daughter?

"I have been so unjust towards you that I can never make amends. When you had gone I realised that your answer to my question was the wisest of all. For your mother and I life had been without taste without you and we have experienced the full truth of what food would be without salt."

And the King said again, "My dear, dear child! What can I give you?"

"You need not give her anything," said the old woman. "I shall give her all the tears she has shed for your sake. They are precious pearls, rarer than those found on the sea bed, and worth more than your entire kingdom. And as payment for her service in my home, I will give her my cottage."

When she said that, she just vanished out of their sight. The little cottage began to shake and the walls rattled and as they looked around them they saw that the little cottage had changed into a magnificent palace. A splendid dinner table stood ready with delicious dishes, and servants ran to and fro ready to serve them.

The flock of geese that had belonged to the old woman were transformed into ladies-in-waiting, ready to obey their new mistress.

The young Count who had been witness to all this did not know what to do when he saw how the little cottage changed. How could he now dare to say what was on his lips as the King called out, "What have I now to give away to my dearest daughter?" Had he lost his chance? Now he stood there quite still, looking at the fair Princess without saying a word.

Then the Queen turned to him saying, "I hope our daughter will not stay here in her palace alone for very long, but will soon be happily married." And the young Count, struggling with words, answered, "From the very first time I saw this lovely Princess and learned of her kindness and wisdom, I knew there could be no other woman in the whole world for me."

The Princess blushed again, but turned to the Count and said jokingly, "When you first set eyes on me, after you helped my dear godmother carry her burden, you hadn't a single word to say, and you even turned your back on me!"

"Yes, you are right," answered the Count, smiling when he remembered his thoughts at the time; and the Princess guessed what he was thinking and smiled back at him.

They all now realised that the old woman was no witch

after all, but a wise fairy who had taught them all a good lesson, and settled their problems happily.

# Martin and Martina
*A story from the Netherlands*

FAR AWAY IN THE ORIENT there lived a mighty king. He had a large kingdom, a wonderful capital with many magnificent palaces and many wives, which was the custom in this part of the world. But there was one thing he did not have and which he wanted more than anything else in the world. This was to have an heir, a son who could take over his large kingdom when it was the will of Allah to call him to his ancestors.

Every morning he prayed to Allah for a son to be born to him. When he was told that his favourite wife was going to have a child, he called an astrologer and asked him if he could see in the stars whether his wife was going to bear him a son.

When the astrologer told him that a son would be born to him there was no end to his rejoicing. But soon his joy changed to darkest despair, for the seer told him that this son would be so beautiful that if the king should ever set eyes on him, he would lose his sight and become a blind man.

The king was terrified that he would become blind, so he

never dared to let his son come before him and sent him away to a desolate old castle, out in the middle of the desert. Here the little prince grew up as the most beautiful child ever seen. He was so lively and active that by the time he was ten years old he spent most of his time wondering how he could escape from this dull life out in the desert.

Once a week there came a caravan of camels loaded with all kinds of goods for the castle. The prince asked his tutor where all these goods came from. He was told that they came from different countries all over the world, to the large port of Basra, and they were then loaded onto this caravan.

One day when all the vessels and bundles had been unloaded at the castle and the caravan was ready to return to Basra, the young prince managed to hide in one of the empty vessels. He arrived at the big port unseen and was able to slip out of the vessel before it was refilled. Then he went about in the harbour looking at the big ships that had come from all corners of the world.

A merchant from the Netherlands caught sight of the handsome boy and asked him where he came from, and who his parents were. The prince told him that his parents were dead, and he had nowhere to go. The merchant asked if he would like to travel about with him, and offered to take care of the boy, and make him his ward. The young prince couldn't think of anything better.

The merchant had the boy christened, gave him the name of Martin and taught him his own language. After some years of travelling in the Orient the merchant decided to return to his home in the Netherlands, and he took Martin with him on a big ship bound for Rotterdam.

Martin did not like his new home-country. He found the sky too grey and heavy, and the people too red-faced and fat.

Besides, they often mocked him for his foreign looks, his slender figure, his black hair, large brown eyes and pale skin. Martin, whose beauty had been acclaimed in his own country, now discovered what it was like to be a foreigner and different from others. Even his foster-father no longer seemed to like him, for when he heard what others thought of his young ward, he kept the boy indoors as much as possible and treated him badly.

Martin tried to bear it, but one day, when the merchant had been rather rough with him, he decided to leave. He wandered about in the woods until dusk, and then, seeing a large, lonely house, he knocked at the door. A young girl with rosy cheeks opened it.

"Please, won't you give a poor traveller shelter for the night?" he asked. "I'm quite exhausted, I've travelled all day, and besides I'm terribly hungry."

"What is your name?" asked the girl.

"My name is Martin," the prince answered.

"Martin!" cried the girl, "isn't that funny, because my name is Martina."

"How extraordinary! Well, surely you can't be so hard-hearted, that you would let me spend the night in the woods?"

"Of course I would like to let you stay here," the girl replied. "But you see, my father is an ogre, and we expect him home any minute." Martin stepped back in fright, but Martina said hurriedly, "Please, do come in anyway, for my mother is friendly and kind and we will find a good hiding place for you."

Martin, who was very hungry, didn't hesitate long, but followed the girl into the house. Martina's mother was really a good woman and welcomed the poor prince most kindly. She gave him as much to eat as he wanted and let him tell her the story of his wanderings. But suddenly there was a terrible bang at the door—the ogre was home.

The wife hurriedly opened the case to the grandfather clock and let the slender boy hide there. Then she went to open the door for her husband. He sat down at the table, for he was always terribly hungry when he returned home in the evening. And he started to eat with a hearty appetite. Suddenly he jumped up from the table and rushed to the clock.

"Who is this that you have hidden from me!" he roared. A corner of Martin's jacket had stuck in the door of the clock case and the ogre had seen it. He went right up to the clock and opened it. But before he had time to do anything, Martina had flung her arms round her father's neck and called out,

"Dear father, don't do him any harm! He is so nice and handsome!"

"He will be nicer still when I've changed him into a goose! Besides he is one of those foreigners I can't stand, and it's quite a while since I had a nice, fine roasted goose."

"Why can't you ever give up that terrible hobby of yours, changing humans into animals? And why are you so keen to use children and young people, especially if they are foreigners? You ought to realise that our daughter is growing up and would like to marry. Whoever do you think would have her as a wife, except, of course, that fat Old William, if you behave like this? Now, when a prince has flopped down here as if he had fallen from the sky, you insist on turning him into a goose and roasting him. You are such a bad father, you really are."

The ogre was not difficult to persuade. He was very impressed at the prospect of being father-in-law to a prince.

"Well," he said, "so you're a prince are you? If you promise to marry my little Martina then I won't turn you into a goose."

Martin had never thought of marrying. He looked at Martina. He didn't think she was particularly pretty, but she was kind, and there was a glint in her eye that attracted him.

Besides, it was nicer to get married than to become a goose and be eaten by her father. So, after a little hesitation, he said, "Yes, I'll marry her."

Martina's face brightened up with happiness. From the first minute she saw the young prince she had liked him, and she detested the fat William, who was a clerk to the Burgomaster of Rotterdam, ugly, mean and old. But it angered the ogre that the prince had hesitated with the answer, so he said to him. "No, my boy, it isn't enough just to say, 'I'll marry her.' I must also know what you are capable of, and you must show me what you are worth."

The poor prince stood there quite stunned. Neither in the old castle in his native country, nor with the merchant had he really learned anything. But he understood it wouldn't do to say so now, so he answered simply, "Tell me only what you want me to do, and I will obey."

"You can go out into the woods tomorrow morning. I want a hundred trees cut down," the ogre answered with a broad smile. "But you may go to bed first, and think matters over."

Little Martina couldn't get a wink of sleep that night, she turned and tossed in her bed. She lay awake thinking of Martin. "The poor boy never will manage a task like that," she thought. "If only my godfather was here! He would have helped us, I know!"

Martina had two mighty godparents. When her father was young, he was a great admirer of the Duke of Brabant who had invented a new kind of beer because of his acquaintance with the fairy of the hops. And when Martina was born her father had done his best to spread the knowledge of this beer, far and wide. As a result these two powerful people came to the christening of his child.

As she could not reach her godfather, she called on her godmother to come and help her. "Come, come my dear God-mother," she called, "Please help to save my betrothed!"

The beautiful fairy suddenly appeared by her bed, tall and slim; she wore a light green dress and a wreath of hop-leaves on her long curly hair. "Are you sure that he really loves you, my dear child?" she asked.

"Well, dear Godmother," Martina burst out, "I pray you, save him all the same! I will love him so much that he will finally return my love."

"May it be according to your wish," the kind fairy said. "Look, here is my magic rod and you may borrow it. It will fulfil all your wishes, but you must make sure nobody takes it from you. And be careful not to lose it!"

Martina thanked her godmother, and at last she was able to sleep.

The old ogre was up early the next morning, and led Martin to a wood in the neighbourhood. He handed him an axe and told him to cut down the trees.

"Set to work, my boy! Three hours is all you have to finish the job, and by then you must have cut down every single tree!" And the ogre smiled and returned home. He sat himself down in an armchair close by the window where he had an excellent view of the wood. And there he sat smoking a pipe while he was watching the trees.

But in the wood poor Martin wandered about with the axe in his hand. He decided it wasn't worthwhile making a single cut, but tried desperately to think of a way to escape from it all. Just then he saw Martina approaching, stealing from tree to tree so as not to be seen by her father.

"Walk in front of me," she said, "so that my father can't see me." Then she touched the trees with her magic rod.

It was wonderful! The trees tumbled down as if they were

32

cut by an axe, with a crash and a thunder. The ogre watching all this from his window, opened his eyes wide in amazement, and his pipe fell from his mouth. It was impossible to understand how this happened. But he was too conceited to show how surprised he was when the prince returned after having finished his job. He said jokingly, "You managed that rather better than I expected. But you have only done a quarter of a day's work. Now you must also dig a fish pond on the spot you have cleared from trees. Let me see you manage that just as well." He had some suspicions, though, and he turned to his daughter saying, "And you my dear girl, can sit here with me and watch."

There was nothing Martin could do but return to the wood alone with a pickaxe on his shoulder. Now he pinned all his hope on Martina, praying that she would be able to help him again. While he was waiting he began poking about with his pickaxe.

Martina sang the most drowsing lullabies she could think of until the old ogre fell asleep, his head nodded, the pipe fell from his mouth, and he began snoring. Then Martina hurried out of the house to Martin in the wood. With a little swing of her wand the place was cleared of all stumps and branches. Then the ground sank down some ten yards and filled with clear water. When the ogre woke up from his nap, Martina was sitting by his side, but when he looked at the place where the wood had been, he was almost dazzled by the glitter from the water in the bright sunshine. He wrinkled his brow with anger and felt thoroughly cheated. During dinner he was in a very bad mood, and seemed to be searching for any excuse to abuse poor Martin.

Finally he brightened up. He had thought of a better plan. "Well, what kind of fish have you put into the pond?" he asked.

"Fish! I never thought of that," Martin stammered, "I just

thought it was the matter of a pond."

The old man felt quite satisfied. Now he was in a good mood again. "You are such a bright fellow! Have you ever heard of a fish-pond without fish?" he chuckled.

"You didn't mention anything about fish, and if he hadn't thought of it himself, it isn't too late for that yet," Martina put in.

"We'll see about that!" said the old tormentor. He sat himself on a terrace outside the house, where he usually had his beer and a nap after dinner. From there he also had an excellent view right over the new pond. "It will be a pleasure to see how he sets about this task." And of course Martina had to follow her father to the terrace and sit by his side. But this time she didn't need to sing to the old man, he fell asleep almost at once.

Immediately, she hurried down to Martin with her wand. But it wasn't too easy to conjure forth fish. She swung her wand in vain, for a long time, but she wouldn't give up. For at least an hour they stood together by the pond trying to conjure up fish, but at last they were successful. The pond began to swarm with fishes of all kinds.

Suddenly a thundering voice rang in the ears of the two young people. "Well you little witch, now I've caught you both red-handed!" roared the ogre, who had sneaked up unseen. He seized them by the ear, one in either hand, and led them back into the house.

"Look here old wife! Now at last, I'll have my roasted goose," he said, and he changed Martin into a goose instantly. His wife, who wanted to gain time and hoped that Martina would find a way to save him, realised she must be careful, so she said, "You are always in such a hurry, can't you at least wait a bit? The day after tomorrow is Sunday, and it would be better to save our nice roast dinner until then."

"Of course, you're right. I will lock up my dainty morsel until then!" And so he locked up the goose in the attic, and there poor Martin could only hope that Martina would come to his rescue.

After supper that night Martina was, as usual, up later than her parents to look after the fire. She took her spinning-wheel, put it in front of the fire-place, touched it with her wand, and said,

"Little spinning-wheel I ask of thee
Don't forget to answer instead of me!"

Then she took a tuft of flax and put it on the first step on the staircase, touched it with her wand and said,

"Little tuft of flax I ask of thee
Don't forget to answer instead of me!"

And then she went upstairs to her little chamber, put a distaff on her bed and said,

"Little distaff I ask of thee
Don't forget to answer instead of me!"

At last she hurried up to the attic. With her wand she touched the door which opened at once, and when she touched the goose, it turned back into her dear Martin. In his delight to have regained his former shape he flung his arms round Martina's neck and gave her a kiss. This made little Martina so happy that she couldn't say a word for quite a while. At last she said, "Now we must flee together, for without the help of my wand you will never be able to escape my father." Martina took Martin by the hand and they both hurried away.

Meanwhile the old ogre lay snoring in his bed. Just before midnight he woke up, and feeling suspicious about his daughter wanted to convince himself that she really had gone to bed.

35

So he roared out in his thunderous voice echoing through the whole house, "Martina, Martina!"

"Here I am, Father," answered the spinning-wheel, "I'm just going to blow out the fire, and will soon go to bed."

Another hour passed, then the old beast woke up again. "Martina, Martina!"

"Here I am, Father," the tuft of flax answered, "I'm just walking up the staircase."

Another hour passed, and the ogre woke up a third time. "Martina, Martina!" he shouted.

"I am in bed, Father," the distaff answered, "Good night!"

"Well, everything is all right," the father murmured, "now I can sleep quietly." And after a while he began snoring again.

But when he woke up next morning to have a look at his Sunday goose, he found it had flown away and so had his daughter. He grunted in fury and disappointment and ordered his poor wife to give him his seven-league boots so that he could catch the fleeing couple.

Martina saw her father running after them from miles away. It would have been quite impossible to escape him. They were standing near one of the many canals in that country, and beside them in the water was a barge. It seemed to be moored to the bank and nobody was on it, so Martina and Martin jumped quickly on board. Martina just had time to change herself to an old woman and Martin to an old man with a long beard, before the old ogre came running along. He stopped in front of the barge and greeting the old couple he said, "You haven't seen a boy with black hair, and a girl in a white dress here in the neighbourhood?"

"Yes, they came walking here along the canal," Martina answered, "in that direction," and she pointed towards the town. Her father set off and reached the town without having seen them. There he thought he had better go and see his old friend Cambrinus, the Duke of Brabant, who was Burgomaster there. The Duke received him very happily, and soon the two old friends sat talking about the old days when they were young. The ogre told his friend about all the hardships he had ·to go through to find his daughter and her friend, and about his failure to trace them.

Cambrinus stroked his beard quietly and said, "Don't work yourself into a passion! One of these days my little god-daughter and her prince will turn up again."

"Do you really think so?"

"Of course. But it's entirely your own fault that they ran away. Why can't you put off that terrible hobby of yours of transforming young people? If you could live as a decent man, I should have offered you an honourable job long ago."

"'What kind of job?" the ogre asked, both flattered and curious.

"Well, my good town here is in need of another Burgomaster as I'm going to retire. I would like to settle in the country, but I need a capable and efficient man as Burgomaster."

The old ogre was a very vain man, and when he heard that he had been considered for Burgomaster, he felt so flattered that he forgot all about the two runaways.

"Yes, I really have considered you," repeated the Duke. "But your awful habit of transforming children and young foreigners into all kinds of animals makes you quite unsuitable for such a post."

The ogre thought matters over for a while, then he burst out, "Isn't there anything else that prevents you appointing me Burgomaster? I promise on my word of honour never to practice my magic power again. It seems that my little witch of a daughter has begun to encroach on my preserves and that simply makes me mad!"

"Well, there you are. Now you've promised me, it's a bargain. I will expect you to dinner here next Sunday, and I will invite the most important persons in the town and solemnly inaugurate you in your official position."

The old ogre really did put off his awful hobby, and became an excellent Burgomaster. For his clerk, he had fat William, Martina's admirer, who was well acquainted with the affairs of the town.

But the new Burgomaster soon had real trouble. The good burghers of the town had grown so fond of the beer invented by Cambrinus, that it was hardly possible to get them out of the beer-houses in the evenings. At eleven when the night-guard called out the time they still sat dozing at their tankards. And in the mornings it was just as difficult to get them out of bed. They didn't hear the chiming of the clock.

The old ogre had become a new and better man now he was Burgomaster, a man who loved law and order. At last he had an excellent idea. "Just wait a little," he thought, "I'll get a bell that will be heard all over the town." From the very best clock-maker in town he ordered a splendid clock, and had it placed in the high tower of the town-hall. Beside the clock a gigantic bell was hung. The clock showed the time very exactly, but someone was also needed to ring the bell at certain hours. Unfortunately this occupation was considered so monotonous that no one wanted to accept it. The Burgomaster and his clerk tried in vain to remedy the matter. To think things over in peace, the Burgomaster took his gun one day, and went out shooting.

He had been out for a couple of hours when he suddenly saw a white spot on the sky. It grew larger as it came nearer and turned out to be a giant swan. He aimed his gun at it and was on the point of shooting, when he heard a voice crying, "Don't shoot, Don't shoot!"

The old ogre was stiff with astonishment, for he recognised his own daughter sitting on the back of the swan. Martina, who had no idea of what had happened while he had been away, was going to find her godfather, Cambrinus, and ask him to help her.

"Get down at once, or I shall shoot!" roared the Burgomaster. The bird sank down to the ground, and Martina jumped down and touched him with her wand. Then the young prince appeared again.

The furious ogre tore the rod out of her hand. But it disappeared immediately and Martina remembered the godmother's warning. Now the poor girl had nothing to protect her betrothed with any longer.

The Burgomaster returned to his town quite upset with the two young people. He was in a terrible mood because he didn't know how to handle this matter. He could, of course, let them marry but he couldn't forgive his daughter. Then fat William suddenly came to his help.

"You need someone to strike the bell," he said, "why not take this young scamp of a boy!"

"What an excellent idea!" exclaimed the Burgomaster.

Poor Martina no longer had her wand to help her dear Martin. He was tied to a pillar beside the clock, high up in the tower, where he could be seen by people on the square below. He was given a hammer to strike every full hour. Fat William made one of his friends a prison warder. The evil clerk smiled contentedly as he thought he could now have Martina's hand in marriage.

But when the Burgomaster passed the town-hall the next day, a large crowd of people had gathered looking up at the

tower. He looked up, and what did he see? Up there stood his own daughter Martina at the side of Martin. He flew into a furious passion. "Well, as the little witch seems to like it so much up there, she may just stay there," he muttered to himself.

And without listening to what other people thought of this, he ordered Martina to be tied on the other side of the large clock. The young couple stood there, exposed to heat and cold. And poor Martina suffered less from her own punishment than from Martin's sufferings. He was totally hidden from her by the large clock, and she couldn't speak to him either, for if she tried the evil warder came out and ordered her to be silent. Martina's selfless love moved the young prince so much that his love for her became equally great.

The burghers of the town were upset at this cruel treatment of the two young people and begged the Burgomaster for mercy. He answered as his evil clerk had suggested, that his daughter was free whenever she would return to her father.

One day it occurred to the Duke Cambrinus to visit his good town and to see how his friend the Burgomaster was getting on. When he passed the square and he heard the clock striking he looked up. Whatever could it be that he could see up there? Wasn't it his own god-daughter?

"What on earth are you doing up there?" he cried up to her.

"Oh! Godfather! Dear, dear Godfather," Martina answered, "here you see the two most unhappy creatures in the world!" and she burst out weeping. At once the evil warder appeared, but a glance from the Duke made him retreat hastily, and Martina was able to tell her whole sad story undisturbed.

Cambrinus went at once to his friend the Burgomaster.

"What foolish things are you up to now?" he asked severely. "How can you let your daughter stand there in the clock tower,

an object of mockery for people? If the children love each other the most reasonable thing is to let them marry."

The Burgomaster had a lot of objections to make, but Cambrinus just made him realise that all of them were nonsense.

"But how on earth can we get on without them? They really keep time excellently, and it was not until I had them here that the burghers would go to bed in time and rise early in the morning."

"Is that your only trouble?" answered Cambrinus, "Then I know a way out. I will get you a pair of mechanical figures made of bronze, which will do this job just as well, and then I will arrange the wedding."

"But what will fat William say to that? I've half promised him the girl in marriage."

"Fat William, that old fool! He has already said too much, and besides, he is in his second childhood. He is only fit for the almshouse." The old ogre changed his ideas at once.

"You are right," he said, "the poor children have been tormented enough." And he sent fat William, and his friend the evil warder, to the almshouse. Cambrinus had two bronze figures made which were placed high up in the tower of the old town-hall, where you can still see them to this day. They were called Martin and Martina after their predecessors.

The very day they were put up in the tower Martin and Martina's wedding was celebrated.

# Zerbino the Solitary
## A story from Italy

IN THE BEAUTIFUL TOWN OF SALERNO there once lived a young woodcutter whose name was Zerbino. His parents were dead, and he had no relatives or friends to care for him and look after him. But every girl in the town longed to share the solitary life of the handsome young man, and were willing to give up all their comforts and money if they could be the wife of the poor woodcutter. They had to be content with only their dreams though, because all their smiles and longing glances were ignored completely by Zerbino.

They grew furious. "He's quite impossible to talk to!" they used to say. "Living on his own has sent him quite crazy." And so they nicknamed him "Zerbino the Solitary".

Early in the morning, when people still lay snoring in their beds, Zerbino took his coat over his arm, and an axe on his shoulder, and went into the woods. There he stayed all day long —not that he was working all the time, the days were much too hot for that—but in the morning he was busy cutting down trees and chopping off their branches and twigs. When the sun was overhead at noon, however, he hung up his coat on a branch and stretched out on the grass in the shade beneath it. He took a little nap and lay for hours watching the birds in the trees and the small ants and beetles on the ground. He learned a lot about the small creatures around him and they all became his little friends.

In the evening he gathered the branches and twigs, cut them into pieces, and tied them together with string into a heavy bundle. Then he went back to town carrying this heavy faggot on his back. In Salerno he plodded from house to house with his bundle, selling wood. When he passed the well where the girls of the town filled their pitchers in the evening, they caught sight of him. "Look, here comes Zerbino the Solitary," the girls whispered to one another. "Let's have a good laugh and tease him a bit!"

"Hello, Zerbino, my darling!" cried one of the girls.

"Look at me, my dear!" another shouted.

"Which of us do you want to marry?" asked a third.

"The one who is able to keep her mouth closed longest," muttered Zerbino, and all the girls burst out laughing.

Such teasing did not exactly encourage Zerbino to seek the company of any of the girls, so when he had finished selling his wood he went straight home. He had a meagre supper of bread and a glass of wine, and then went to bed, a poor straw-bed, but he could go to sleep quite happily for he was free to do what he wanted and had no worries in the world.

One day at noon, when Zerbino was looking, as usual, for a cool, pleasant spot for his siesta, he wandered into a leafy glade, with tall trees clustered round a pool. He was just about to settle down when he discovered, asleep in the grass, the loveliest maiden he had ever seen. Her dress was of swansdown and on her hair she wore a wreath of fragrant flowers. But she seemed to be having a restless dream for her face was screwed up, and her hands were twitching.

"Is this good sense? To sleep with the sun straight into one's face like this?" muttered Zerbino. So he hung his coat on some branches of the tree above the pretty maiden so that she lay in the shade. Just then, he discovered a poisonous snake close by the girl. With its head upright, the snake slithered nearer and nearer to her. Zerbino saw the forked tongue flickering to and fro, and was aware instantly of its evil wishes.

"Oh, you monster! So small and yet so evil!" Zerbino said. "You certainly don't belong to my small animal friends!" He lifted his axe and cut the dangerous snake into pieces. But the pieces still twitched along the ground as if they wanted to hurt the sleeping girl and Zerbino lifted his foot and kicked them with all his force right into the pool. As they splashed into the water there was a hissing sound as if they were pieces of red-hot iron.

At this sound the beautiful girl woke up, rose from the grass, and cried full of delight: "Oh, Zerbino! Zerbino, my dear!"

"What? You too! Are you making the same fuss as the rest of the girls? I thought you, at least, would be different," muttered Zerbino angrily.

"My poor boy, of course I'm different. I only wanted to thank you for having saved my life."

"I haven't saved your life at all," muttered Zerbino, "but just be careful you don't go to sleep another time without looking round first to see if there is a dangerous snake in the neighbourhood. Well, that's my advice. Now, goodbye, I must be off. I haven't time to waste for I'm going to have my siesta."

"But wait a minute, I want to reward you for the favour you did me. You haven't only saved my life, you have also killed my bitterest enemy. That snake was a terrible, cruel ogre who wanted to marry me. And ever since the day when I told him how I detested him, and could never become his wife, he has been pursuing me disguised as all kinds of dangerous animals trying to kill me. Haven't you any wish I could grant in return?" asked the girl, for she was really a fairy and had all sorts of magic powers.

"Well yes, to be left alone," Zerbino said stretching himself out in the grass. "If you don't want anything, you've got what you want. And when you've got what you want you are happy!" Zerbino concluded his talk and turned over on the other side to go to sleep.

"My poor Zerbino, you are in a bad state. 'When you've got what you want, you are happy!' These were your own words, dear Zerbino. Well, now I know what your reward will be. You shall have everything you wish for, and there will come a time when you will remember me with gratitude," said the fairy, and disappeared like a sunbeam.

After a few hours rest Zerbino rose to continue his work. He cut all the branches and twigs into pieces, and then he tied the pieces together into a large faggot. When he sat astride the faggot, tightening the last knot on the string which held the wood together, he felt very tired.

"Oh," he said with a sigh, "now I have to carry this faggot to town. What a pity it can't carry me instead! Faggots like this ought to have legs. I just wish they had so that I could ride home to Salerno like a noble prince."

He had hardly finished his wish, when he felt the faggot lift itself under him on four twig-legs and set off at full trot.

Zerbino almost fell off in astonishment, but he soon calmed down and seizing the string with one hand, like a rein, while he proudly held the axe over his shoulder with the other, he rode along in fine style. Everyone he passed turned round to stare in amazement at the strange rider on his queer horse.

In those days a royal palace stood in the large square of Salerno and the King used to spend part of every year at this lovely town. Then the townsfolk could see the King's daughter, the Princess Aleli, on one of the balconies, surrounded by her ladies-in-waiting. And the town was crowded with noble knights and foreign princes, who had all come to the court to ask for the Princess's hand in marriage. But the beautiful Aleli had dismissed every one of them. She was bored to tears hearing them constantly flattering her. They spoke admiringly of "her wonderful beauty, her brilliant wit, and her noble manners," but all the time the Princess thought: "It isn't me they want, it's the town of Salerno which my father has promised as a dowry to the one who marries me."

And the Princess grew sadder and sadder, and people said that the poor Princess had entirely forgotten how to laugh.

This same evening the Princess seemed even more grave and sad than usual when Zerbino suddenly appeared in the square as proud as any noble knight, riding along on his queer horse of twigs and branches with his axe over his shoulder. At this sight the ladies-in-waiting burst into a roar of laughter, and clapped their hands and threw flowers at him. One of them, who had no flowers handy, even threw an orange which hit Zerbino in the middle of his face.

"Keep laughing, you nitwits!" the furious woodcutter cried out, shaking his fist at them. "I wish that you would go on laughing until your teeth drop out. That is just what you deserve!"

And now the ladies-in-waiting laughed more than ever before. The Princess, who thought it unworthy of their high rank, tried in vain to stop them, and looked quite desperate.

47

"Poor little Lady," Zerbino said to the Princess, "how grave and sad you look. I wish that you would fall in love with the first man who makes you laugh and brightens up your dull and gloomy life. And may you marry him as well," he added as if to assure her happiness.

Now the proud rider wanted to set off at full speed again, and so he pulled the string with all his might, quite forgetting that it was not the reins of a real horse. But this was something he should not have done, for the string slipped off the faggot and all the twigs fell flat to the ground, with Zerbino on top, flat on his back with his legs high up in the air.

At this the gloomy Princess herself could not help laughing. And then she looked at Zerbino, quite surprised that she had not realised before what a wonderful man he was. She stood for a while gazing at him, giving him longing glances without noticing that her ladies were still roaring with laughter around her.

She watched Zerbino admiringly while he carefully tied his twigs into another faggot. Then, quite unaware of the commotion he had caused at the royal palace, Zerbino went home as usual to his humble supper and his poor straw bed.

While these strange things were happening the King sat in council with his ministers. But hardly had the council broken up and the King retired to his private rooms, when his daughter came running in to him. She flung her arms round his neck, sobbing bitterly.

"Darling, what is the matter? Is there anything you want?" asked the King surprised. "You know there isn't anything in the world I would deny you. Speak out, my dear!"

"No, it really isn't anything special. It's just the very thing you have asked me to do many times before. I am fulfilling *your* wish instead. At last I've found the man I want to marry."

"I must say, this is good news. I'm delighted you have got rid of your foolish ideas about not getting married. By the way, who is he? That is the important thing and you've quite forgotten to tell me."

When the Princess remained silent, the King went on, "Come now, my dear, don't be shy! Is it the Prince of Spain? The Duke of Palermo? Perhaps it is the Baron of Cava?"

But the Princess only shook her head to every name.

"Who on earth is it then?" asked the King at last.

"Father I can't tell you because I don't know who he is."

"Do you really mean to say you don't even know the name

of the man you want to marry? But you have seen him, haven't you?"

"Oh yes, of course, right here in the square."

"Did you speak to him?"

"No, but I knew at once that he was the only husband for me. No one else in the whole world could replace him."

"My dear child, this is indeed a very serious matter. It's not your private affair, you know, he must at least be a man of noble family."

"I don't know anything about his family, but what does that matter when I know I love him, and have made up my mind to marry him?"

"Nonsense, my girl, a king's daughter just can't marry anyone, least of all a commoner."

"I don't care a bit about being a king's daughter. And didn't you say yourself just now that you would do anything for me?" said Aleli beginning to cry again.

"Do stop making such a fool of yourself. We may yet find out who this gentleman is whom you don't know, and haven't even spoken to. Where does he live?"

"I really can't tell," answered the Princess.

"My poor child, I think you have gone quite crazy. Get these ridiculous ideas out of your head!" he said and ordered the Princess's ladies-in-waiting to come and take her to her bedroom and help her to bed.

The ladies came before the King, still roaring with laughter.

"Have you all gone mad! Stop that disrespectful laughing at once!" roared the King angrily.

But alas, the poor ladies could not stop themselves, they just fell in a heap, shrieking and giggling. Then the King called the guards and ordered them to throw all the ladies in prison. "In there," he said sternly, "they may go on laughing to their heart's content."

But then the ladies' laughter gasped to a halt and they fell on their knees in remorse, promising the King that they would never laugh again for the rest of their lives. For while they had been doubled up with mirth, every single tooth in their heads had fallen out. They were certain it was the work of that terrible magician who had come galloping through the town on a faggot.

"Now I am certain that you have all taken leave of your senses! A galloping faggot! What nonsense! A magician! Magicians don't exist. I don't believe in them."

"Oh but they do, they do, we have seen one! We all saw him right here in the square outside the palace. When a man is trotting along on a faggot as if it were a horse, what else could he be but a magician?"

"Hmm," said the King, "Riding about on a faggot, was he? That certainly seems rather suspicious, I must say."

He told the guards to set the ladies free, and ordered them instead to set out and find the magician on the faggot.

"May he be tied to his faggot and burned at the stake with it, so that at last I shall have peace in my own palace," said the King.

But then it seemed as if the Princess really had lost her senses. She wrung her hands in despair, and wailed at the top of her voice: "You mustn't burn my sweetheart! You mustn't burn my sweetheart! I'm going to marry that noble rider on the faggot. He is my chosen fiancé. If you kill him, you can kill me as well!"

"I think my whole court must be bewitched!" cried the poor King. What was he to do? As usual, when the King was at a loss he called his Prime Minister. "He ought to solve my problems, what else is a Prime Minister here for?" thought the

King to himself.

The Minister came rushing in, a little, fat man with a long nose and three chins. He smiled fawningly and looked very conceited.

"Here you are at last! What on earth is going on in my kingdom?"

"Your Majesty, everything is in perfect order," said the Minister quietly, making a deep bow.

"You are supposed to be my minister and you don't even know what is happening in my kingdom. A magician is riding about the town and has bewitched my whole court, and on top of it all my daughter wants to marry him. Yet you say that everything is in perfect order!"

"Of course I knew all about *that*," said the Minister soothingly, "But I didn't think it worth mentioning."

"And you know where this scoundrel is right now, do you?" asked the King.

"Of course, your Majesty," answered the Minister with the same smiling expression on his lips, though he felt anything but easy.

"Well then, bring him here within an hour, without fail." With grace and charm, and self-centred rippling through every muscle, the Minister bowed his way from the room.

But hardly had the palace gate closed behind him than he flew into a passion. His face grew quite red and he could hardly draw breath.

Why on earth should the King make *him* responsible for this? He set off to the Mayor of the town. "What is the point in having a Mayor, if he doesn't know what is going on in town?" he thought.

"My Lord Mayor, if you don't bring me the man who is riding about town on a faggot within a quarter of an hour, you may consider yourself dismissed from your post," he snarled angrily.

Perplexed, the Mayor rose from his chair, anxious to get some further details about the matter, but the Minister had already stormed from the room. "Well," he thought to himself, "it's not my job to arrest scoundrels, what's the Chief of Police for?" So he set off to find the Chief of Police.

"There is a man riding about on a faggot, who is the most dangerous scoundrel in this kingdom, and if you don't bring him to the King within ten minutes it will be your last day as Chief of Police," the Mayor snapped to the Chief of Police.

The Chief of Police grew very alarmed, and at once called all his police force together. "Go out and find that scoundrel on the faggot, and bring him to the royal palace within five minutes," were his orders.

As soon as the policemen came out into the street, they grabbed the first boy they set eyes on, and asked him where they could find the man who was riding about on a faggot.

To ride about on such an extraordinary horse as a bundle of twigs has its risks, for by now there wasn't a single streetboy in the town of Salerno who didn't know Zerbino and where he lived.

Meanwhile, at the palace, the King was at a loss to know what to do. It wasn't every day that he was in a position to offer his subjects the spectacle of burning a magician at the stake, but when he saw how it was driving his daughter to despair, he hesitated. The ladies-in-waiting had tried in vain to persuade the Princess to retire to her rooms. There was no-one who was able to sooth her feelings.

The Minister, who had now returned to the palace, made a sign to the King as if there was a secret arrangement between them. He stepped forward to the Princess, bowed low, and said in honeyed tones: "Your Royal Highness, your fiancé will soon be here. Wipe away your tears and follow your ladies. Let them help you to put on the most becoming of your dresses and the most precious of your jewels, so that you can receive him looking as beautiful as ever."

"Oh, now I understand!" cried Aleli. "Dear, dear father, a thousand thanks!" And she embraced her father and left the room, radiant with joy. When she caught sight of a courtier outside the door she told him that her fiancé was soon to arrive at the palace and he should see that this noble man should have a worthy reception.

Hardly had Aleli shut the door after her, than the King turned furiously on the Minister.

"What on earth do you mean by this? Have you taken leave of your senses? I am the King here, you know, and you would do well to remember it."

"Oh, Your Majesty, how can anyone see tears in the Princess's beautiful eyes, and the agony in her lovely face without soothing her sorrow? And that I felt was most important at the moment," answered the Minister with his usual fawning smile.

"Have you forgotten that I have ordered the magician to be burnt at the stake? And a King's order must be carried out promptly."

"Well, that's true, Your Majesty, but you have now also promised that the Princess can marry this man. A King, Your Majesty, must keep his promise, so why not marry the Princess —quite secretly of course—to the magician, and let him be burnt at the stake afterwards. That way you won't break any of your promises and justice will be done too."

"Oh Minister! You are the most wonderful of scoundrels!" cried the King.

"No, Your Majesty, you are exaggerating. I'm only a Minister," answered the Minister, smiling with delight.

Aleli returned, more lovely than the King had ever seen her before and shining with joy. The King look admiringly at his daughter and couldn't help hoping that the man on the faggot turned out to be a prince after all, or at least a mighty nobleman, for then, of course, he wouldn't have to be burned.

The police found their way easily to Zerbino's humble home. They ordered him to come out at once, and fell upon him, pulling his arms, punching his back and kicking his legs.

"What do you want with me?" Zerbino asked frankly, knowing that his conscience was clear.

"Silence, you scoundrel! We have orders to bring you before the King," the men informed him.

"I wish you were in my shoes," said Zerbino angrily when he saw one of the policemen raising his fist ready to box his ear. Surprisingly, the man then missed Zerbino and hit one of his own friends instead, right in the middle of his face. A general fight broke out amongst the police force and no-one had time to look after their prisoner. Zerbino didn't care what became of his guardians, he set out by himself towards the royal palace.

On his arrival he was met by a group of courtiers who were sent out to receive him according to the orders of the Princess. They greeted him cordially and doffed their hats almost to the ground. Zerbino politely returned their greetings. But when the courtiers went on bowing and sweeping their hats off he thought they were pulling his leg, and said angrily: "I have had enough of your greetings, why not have some dancing for a change?"

At once the courtiers began to dance, swinging their hats in the air. It was indeed a ridiculous sight. Zerbino was shown into the large audience hall and entered it followed by the dancing courtiers. There sat the King with the Princess Aleli at his side, looking her very best. She rose from her seat and stepped forward to greet her fiancé when he entered.

"Father," she called out, "here is the noble man you have chosen to become my husband. Even if he isn't a Prince by birth, he is more worthy and more handsome than other men. And I know that I shall be happier with him than with any other man in the whole world."

The King was too upset to find words for his daughter's shameless behaviour. He only turned his head towards his Minister and glanced helplessly at him.

The Minister, always ready to help his King, stepped forward bravely and spoke in a harsh voice to the woodcutter.

"Speak up now and tell us who the deuce you are, a disguised Prince or a magician?"

"I'm no more a magician than you, fatty," answered Zerbino rudely. At this cheeky reply the Minister lost his temper.

"Your Majesty," he bellowed, "let justice be done, burn that magician, that wizard, that scoundrel, that . . ."

"Oh, that's right, keep bellowing and barking, silly old man!" interrupted Zerbino. And instead of finishing the sentence the Minister started to roar like a lion and bark like a dog.

Both Zerbino and Princess Aleli, who now had taken his arm, burst out laughing. The King could hardly control himself any longer.

"Get out of here!" he shouted to Zerbino and Aleli. "Guard, seize them both! See they are married at once and throw them into a boat in the harbour. They can sail away to a foreign country and take care of themselves as best they can. I don't want to see them any more!"

But when the King saw how happily Aleli went to share

Zerbino's fate, gloomy though it seemed to be, he took pity on her.

"My poor daughter, what will become of you with no one at your side but that man?" he thought.

"Guard!" he suddenly called out, "See that the Minister accompanies them. After all, it might be some consolation for the Princess to have a clever man at her side who can give her a good piece of advice now and then."

This came as a bolt from the blue to the Minister. He tried his utmost to resist the guard, but nothing could prevent the King's faithful soldier from carrying out the royal order.

So the poor Minister was dragged away. First he had to witness the wedding, then he was thrown into a boat with the newly married couple. Soon the three of them were floating about on the high seas in a poor little vessel.

Luckily there was a soft breeze, and the night was fine with a bright moon and twinkling stars. Zerbino sat at the helm, humming a song, with Aleli at his side. She seemed quite happy with her fate. But at the bottom of the boat lay the Minister hurling a torrent of abuse upon Zerbino.

"What are we going to do now, you miserable magician, you lousy wizard, you ignorant fool?"

But Zerbino did not even listen to him, he only went on singing. Suddenly he stopped and said he felt hungry and would have liked some figs and raisins. And from nowhere there seemed to fall a box of figs right down at the feet of the astounded Minister. It was immediately joined by a box of raisins.

"Well, now I know your secret Mr Zerbino! But you don't seem to know it yourself," thought the Minister, "I shall certainly know how to make best use of it. First of all though, I must win the favour of Zerbino and his Princess." He took the two boxes and handed them to Zerbino, made a deep bow and said smilingly, "Here you are, Your Grace. As you see I'm ready to fulfill even your slightest wish. Please do forget the silly things I said before, I didn't mean them at all. I must have had an attack of dizziness, I'm not a very good sailor, you see."

Zerbino took the boxes, glad to have something to eat and asked his wife to share the raisins and figs, while the untiring Minister went on talking.

"Do you remember, Your Grace, your wedding was only a few hours ago? Why don't you give your royal bride a suitable present?"

"Do stop talking, fatty! I'm dead tired of hearing your voice. Where do you think I should get this present from? From the bottom of the sea perhaps? Well then, you may dive down there and ask the fish for a precious jewelled necklace."

Hardly had he spoken than the Minister was flung overboard by invisible hands and disappeared under the waves.

A few minutes later the Minister re-appeared. He emerged from the depths with water streaming down his face, hardly able to draw breath. But a wonderful diamond jewel sparkled between his teeth like a star in the night. Zerbino grabbed him by his hair and dragged him into the boat. As soon as the Minister was able to speak again, he said: "This is a wedding present to the beautiful Princess Aleli from the fish. As you see, Your Grace, I'm keeping my word. I've now given you another proof of how faithfully I'm going to serve you."

But Zerbino and Aleli didn't listen to the poor man, they were busy eating their figs and raisins.

"Your Grace," said the Minister after a short pause, "don't you care at all for your poor wife? This miserable, small boat may capsize at any moment, and what will then become of the noble Lady? She ought to have a vessel better fitting her high rank. Your Highness," he said turning to Aleli, "don't you remember the beautiful ship the Prince of Spain sent to Salerno? It was entirely of mahogany, with silken sails and cabins and large rooms: it glittered of gold and ivory everywhere. And don't you remember the fine drawing-room with mirrors covering the walls from ceiling to floor? That was indeed a royal ship! And Mr Zerbino, you who are a mighty and noble gentleman ought not to have anything less magnificent to offer your wife."

"I'm feeling quite comfortable here," said Zerbino. And he thought to himself, "What a funny old chap he is, his mouth rattles away like a mill-clapper. I wish I did have a ship like that, if only to keep his mouth shut just for a moment."

Immediately Zerbino and Aleli sat up rubbing their eyes. Their little boat now grew in all directions and was filled with many wonderful things. Large silken sails swelled out in the soft breeze, and the ship floated proudly ahead like a swan on the waves.

The Minister ran about to find one of the crew to whom he could give orders. But alas, he could not find a single soul either on deck or below it. So he was as lonely as usual. When he felt like talking to someone he had to address Zerbino or Aleli. He went up on deck and bowing low to Zerbino he said,

"Your Grace, I hope you are satisfied with my duties?"

"Be quiet, you chatterbox!" answered Zerbino, "I wish you would keep your tonque quiet till to-morrow morning, so that we can be left in peace for a while."

The Minister went sullenly down below deck where he found the dining-room. The table was spread with a fine meal. He sat down and ate and drank to his heart's content. The wine was, in fact, so excellent that he drank rather too much, and after a while he felt dizzy and sank down on his chair asleep.

Zerbino and Aleli remained on deck enjoying the wonderful voyage on their magic ship. Even Zerbino began to appreciate the company of his lovely wife as she stood at his side listening to the wind rustling in the silken sails and looking out over the glittering waves.

Next morning the Minister woke up feeling life was very dull without a single soul to talk to. What on earth could he do on a ship without a crew! If only he could make his master wish himself ashore. But he knew he had to be careful, or he would perhaps be sent down to the bottom of the sea again or somewhere even worse.

When the Minister came up on deck again, he found Zerbino and Aleli talking gaily together. He heard Aleli saying how lovely it would be to live alone with her dear husband, even if they couldn't afford anything else other than a little cottage for themselves and a cow. That was all she wanted.

When the Minister heard these words he shivered with fear. This must be prevented at all costs.

"Your Highness!" he cried out desperately at the top of his voice, "Can't you see the wonderful palace over there?"

"No, I can't," answered Aleli quietly.

"Can't you really see it? It is of white marble, surrounded with green parks and gardens and there you could really feel at home. It's even larger and more comfortable than your father's palace. Wouldn't that suit you better than a little hut?"

"No, in a palace there are courtiers and servants and they never leave you alone."

"Then a little cottage is much better," said Zerbino. Now fear increased the Minister's power of invention.

"Oh," he cried, "that palace isn't an ordinary one. There are neither courtiers nor servants. There you can be left alone and yet will be served, for the furniture has legs and the walls have ears."

"Have they got tongues as well?" asked Zerbino.

"Oh yes they have, and they can tell you everything you wish—but they can keep quiet too," he added hurriedly.

"Then they are wiser than you. That is exactly the palace for me. Let's sail up to it." Zerbino called out.

"Look! Look! There it is! cried the Princess pointing to an island which suddenly emerged on the surface of the sea. In the middle of the island was a huge, marble palace surrounded by lovely gardens and parks.

The magic ship steered into a creek, and the three people on board jumped ashore. The Minister hurried ahead to the palace and ran up the broad marble steps leading up to a high porch. He knocked at the door, and a voice answered: "What do you want, stranger?"

"I should like to talk to the owner of this palace," answered the Minister.

"The owner is Mr Zerbino," said the door.

When Zerbino and Aleli came up the steps, the door opened by itself. They entered into a magnificent hall from where they wandered into large rooms and fine halls, admiring all the beautiful things they saw.

"How beautiful it is in here!" said the Princess, "but where are the chairs?"

"We must have chairs to sit on!" cried Zerbino.

"Here we are, here we are!" said some soft voices, and in came the chairs, running in a row, one after the other.

"Wouldn't it be lovely to have some breakfast now?" asked the Minister.

"Oh yes it would, but we must have a table!" said Zerbino.

"Here I am!" shouted a deep voice, and a table came walking solemnly into the hall.

"How thrilling!" said Aleli enthusiastically, "but where is the food then?"

"Yes, some food would taste excellent, just now," remarked Zerbino.

"Here we are, here we are!" squeaked the plates and dishes dancing upon the table. They were filled with an assortment of delicious food and soon all three of the small company were having a hearty meal.

"Mr Zerbino!" the Minister called out, "now you see what I have done for you! All this is my work."

"You are a liar!" a voice called out. It was the wall that had spoken.

"Your Grace, don't believe such slander, I never tell a lie," the Minister said, a bit ashamed.

"You are a liar!" This time the voice came from the ceiling.

"Wouldn't it be nicer to have some company here? You could become a King surrounded by gay courtiers, soldiers, and other people who could pay you homage and obey your orders. And I could become your Minister then," he concluded hopefully.

"Oh, please don't take any notice of his chatter," Princess Aleli whispered. "It's wonderful to be here. Don't you think we could stay here?" The Minister, who heard the Princess's words, said: "Yes, of course it's wonderful here, that's exactly what I think too."

"You are a liar," a voice said again.

"Can't you ever stop lying!" Zerbino cried angrily. "Fly away to the moon so that I can be rid of your eternal chatter at last."

This wish was a bit too hasty, for as soon as he said it the poor Minister flew out of the room, up in the air and disappeared in the sky. And that was the last that was ever seen of him.

Aleli and Zerbino, however, lived happily in their magic palace and Zerbino realised at last the wonderful power the fairy had given him, and remembered her with gratitude.

After some time Zerbino and Aleli wished their magic ship to bring them to the old King. They paid him a short visit to tell him how happy they both were in their magic palace. The old King, who had often regretted his harshness to his daughter, was very pleased to hear about her happiness. He promised to

pay them a visit to see their wonderful palace. He understood that he could never have offered his daughter anything better than her present life, alone with the man she loved, in a palace where the furniture had legs and the walls had ears, and she was able to have every wish fulfilled.

# Marc the Rich and Vasilij the Unfortunate

*A story from France, based on the original by Perrault*

LONG AGO there lived a merchant whose name was Marc. He was one of the richest people in the country and was known to everyone as Marc the Rich. A fleet of fine ships sailing on the large rivers belonged to him, and many estates and villages of peasants were under his allegiance. In the big cities he had large store-houses filled with precious goods from all parts of the world, and his palace was filled with treasures. Soft carpets covered the floors, beautiful tapestries hung on the walls, and every room shimmered and glittered with silver and gold.

Marc himself was a hard and cruel man, mean and intolerant to everyone he met. Sick and poor people who came under this window to beg were driven away by his servants with orders from Marc to set the dogs on them. There was only one living person whom Marc loved and whose slightest wish he gladly granted, and that was his little three-year-old daughter, Anastasia.

One day when it was very cold and a fierce wind was blowing, three old men came walking up to the house. They looked lean and haggard, and their worn, thin clothes hung in rags and tatters. But their long, white beards and white hair gave their ancient wrinkled faces a wise and almost venerable appearance. They stopped under Marc's window shivering with cold, their long beards tossing about in the wind. They begged Marc to give them some kind of shelter, however simple, for the night.

Just as Marc was giving orders to his servants to set the fierce dogs on them, little Anastasia, who was standing at his side, said, "Can't you see, Father, how they are shivering? Can't you let them stay in the barn for the night?"

Marc was quite surprised at such a request from his child, but of course he could not resist her, and he let her have her own way. Instead of setting the dogs on the three old men, the servants had to show them to the barn. Anastasia seemed to have taken a fancy to the men. Unnoticed, the little girl stole after them to the barn. She climbed up to the loft from where she could look down at them secretly. She saw how the old men tried to make themselves comfortable in the straw, and how their shrivelled hands no longer shook with cold. After a while they began talking to each other.

"What news from the wide world?" asked the eldest of the three. Without hesitation the second answered, "In the little village of Fatjanovo, in the hut of Ivan the Poor, a seventh son has been born this night. What are we going to call him? And what kind of christening-gift shall we give him?"

The third man considered the matter for a moment, then he said, "We are going to call him Vasilij, and we shall present him with the whole fortune of Marc the Rich."

As soon as little Anastasia heard this she stole out of the loft again, and went into the house to tell her father what the old men had said. At first Marc laughed at her and said that she could not possibly have understood anything of their conversation. But he decided he had better go to the barn to find out if there could be any truth in it.

"Could these men really be so ungrateful? Haven't I given them shelter as they asked? Is this how they thank me?" he thought to himself.

But when he came to the barn there was not the slightest sign of the three old men. They had just vanished, and no-one had seen a sign of them. Marc felt uneasy and that night he didn't get a wink of sleep. Early next morning he ordered his coach and horses, and drove to the village of Fatjanovo.

"I really must find out whether a child was born here last night," he thought. He went to the parish church and asked the parson about Ivan the Poor and his family. The parson answered, "Ivan is indeed the poorest of all the poor peasants in this village. A seventh son was born to him just last night. He lives in a hut of clay, and its floor is nothing but hard-trodden earth. He is so poor that no one wants to become the godfather of the new-born child."

When he heard this Marc the Rich became even more uneasy than he had been before. He remembered what his little daughter had told him about the prophecy of the three old beggars. Then he suddenly declared, "If no one else wants to become the poor child's godfather I shall do so myself."

The parson was astonished. Could this really be Marc the Rich of whom so many stories of cruelty and meanness were told? When Marc asked the parson to set up a fine table and arrange a christening party at his expense, he became even more convinced that all the stories he had heard were untrue. He went at once and told his wife about the arrangements. The parson's wife decided then to become the child's godmother.

When all the preparations were finished the parson went to

Ivan the Poor's hut to fetch the baby and its father and bring them to the church for the christening ceremony.

At the meal Marc the Rich spoke many a friendly word to Ivan the Poor. "My dear friend," he said, "you are a poor man and can't afford to give your son a good education. Give him to me, and I shall care for him the rest of his life, and on top of that, I will give you a thousand roubles to make your own life easier."

Ivan thought the matter over for a moment, and finally admitted that this was the very best thing that could happen to his new-born son. Yes, even his wife had to agree to this, and there seemed nothing wrong about that. So he accepted the money and gave away his son. Marc also gave a sum of money to the child's godmother, as was the custom. Then he wrapped the baby in a fox fur, lifted it up in his coach and drove away.

When he had driven about ten miles, he passed a steep cliff at the road side. Marc told the driver to stop. He picked up the child, went to the edge of the cliff and threw him over.

"Now you go ahead and take all my riches!" he cried out. With a light heart Marc the Rich continued his journey home.

Shortly after Marc had left the site of his evil deed, two merchants came riding along the road. They were just on their way to Marc the Rich with some goods. As they were passing the cliff one of them suddenly halted saying, "Stop a minute! Can't you hear something crying?"

"Nonsense, you must have heard the call of a bird," answered the other and wanted to continue his ride. But the one who had spoken first went to the edge of the cliff, and could then quite clearly hear the sound of a baby crying. Peering over the edge of the cliff he caught sight of a bundle hanging from a bush that grew in a crevice on the steep rock below. The crying sound was coming from the bundle. Now he called his friend and the two of them managed to scramble down and grasping the bundle, found inside—a little new-born baby. They wrapped the tiny, crying creature in some furs which were among the goods intended for Marc the Rich and went on their way.

When they arrived at Marc's house they told Marc about their remarkable discovery. Marc realised at once that the little baby was none other than his new godson.

"Let me see him," he urged. And they brought the child to him. "Let me have him for my own son, and I shall take care of him for the rest of his life," said Marc, "and I shall give you a thousand roubles as well." The merchants agreed to the bargain deciding that, after all, Marc the Rich must be kinder than his reputation. So they left his home quite content.

As soon as the merchants departed, Marc looked round quickly and wondered how on earth he could get rid of this troublesome baby now. In his room he found a little wooden box where he kept some unimportant things. He emptied it and put the baby inside. Then he went down to a large river and threw the box into the water.

The wooden box drifted with the current, and finally stuck on the bank far down the river. Near by there was a monastery and a couple of monks were down on the bank busily drying their fishing tackle. Suddenly they heard the crying of a child. Surprised, they looked round and saw a wooden box floating on the water, from which came the sound of crying. They grabbed hold of the box and opened it, to discover they hadn't been mistaken for inside they found a new-born baby. When the abbot saw the baby and heard how he had been found, he decided that the child should stay with them in the monastery. He took it for granted that the baby wasn't christened, so the child was christened a second time and they gave him the name "Vasilij", adding to it "the unfortunate", as the poor little thing had been abandoned so pitilessly by its parents.

From that day Vasilij lived in the monastery. He grew up into a fine and handsome youth with a gentle heart and a quick brain, dearly loved by the abbot and the monks. They taught him to read and write and he became a great help to them in many ways. But there was one thing above all that he loved doing and he also did better than anyone else, and that was to play the organ and to sing. He did it so well that the abbot made him the leader of the boy's choir and the cantor of the church.

As the years passed by and Marc the Rich grew older he remained the same mean and intolerant man as before. But one day he fell ill, and he began to consider the many sins he had on his conscience.

"If ever I get well again, I shall give a large sum of money to a church or monastery," he promised, "so that they may pray for my soul and secure me a place in heaven before it's too late."

Marc the Rich was cured, and set out again as usual, on his long business tours. Sailing along the river on one of his ships he passed a monastery on the river-bank. Remembering his promise he decided to go ashore to see the abbot. He talked with him and gave him a large sum of money, saying that he wanted also to see the church and attend Mass there.

He heard the abbot calling a young man to tell him to lead the choir. When Marc saw the young handsome youth who carried out the orders so promptly he turned to the abbot and asked, "Has this young man stayed here with you for very long? He seems to be quite at home with his work. Who is he?"

"Well, let me see! It's about nineteen years now since we found a wooden box floating on the river with a tiny new-born baby inside. We took care of him and called the poor child Vasilij the Unfortunate. He has stayed with us ever since, and we haven't once had the slightest cause to regret it, for he has always been such a source of pleasure to us," replied the abbot.

Marc gave a start. "How odd," he thought, "Vasilij? Isn't that the name I gave my godson whom I have thought dead for so long? Nineteen years ago—the wooden box—Vasilij, it all fits in. There is no doubt, this youth is my own godson." Aloud he said, "He seems to me the very man I'm looking for. I want to put all my wealth in charge of a man I can trust and make him a warden of all my estates and store-houses. You probably know how much I possess, don't you?"

The abbot was by no means willing to let Vasilij go and had quite a lot of excuses to make. But when Marc promised a gift of ten thousand roubles to the monastery, the abbot said he wanted to think the matter over. The abbot consulted the monks to get their advice. "Why," they said, "shall we stand in the way of Vasilij and prevent him making his fortune? Let Marc the Rich make him a warden of all his goods; Vasilij will certainly be far better off with him than with us and the life we can offer him here in the monastery." So it was decided to send Vasilij the Unfortunate with Marc the Rich.

Marc told Vasilij to go on board one of his ships that lay at anchor in the river and was to leave for his home in a few hours. He himself was going to continue his journey in the other direction to a country far away, and was glad, he said, to have a man at home whom he could trust. Marc also gave Vasilij a letter which he was to deliver to Marc's wife.

This was the letter Marc wrote:

*"Dear Wife,*

*When the deliverer of this letter comes to you, go with him to our soap factory under pretence of showing him around. When you pass the large boiling pot, you must push him into it. If you don't obey orders, you will be severely punished, for you must realise that this youth is the worst of my enemies."*

It was signed with Marc's name and sealed.

Vasilij took the letter, said goodbye to the abbot and the monks, and went down to the ship. He felt a bit ashamed that he wasn't quite so sorry as he ought to be at leaving the monastery which had been his home for such a long time, and the kind monks who had been so good to him. He couldn't deny that he was thrilled with hopes of the new life that lay ahead of him.

"What adventures shall I meet in the wide world that now lies open to me?" he thought as he went ashore and walked up towards Marc's magnificent house, carefully holding the letter to Marc's wife in his hand. Suddenly he caught sight of three old and venerable men with white hair and long white beards. They walked straight up to him, stopped and asked, "Where are you going, Vasilij the Unfortunate?" Vasilij looked up surprised at hearing his full name spoken by strangers. "Well," he answered, "I'm going to the house of Marc the Rich where I am to deliver a letter to his wife."

"Will you please show us the letter?" said the man who seemed to be the oldest. Vasilij then handed him the letter. Each one of the three took the letter in his hand and breathed on it. When it was handed back to Vasilij, the old man said, "Well then, go ahead, young man, and hand over this letter to the wife of Marc the Rich, and may God bless you."

When Vasilij arrived at the house, he found it more splendid than he ever had imagined. He was at once shown into the room of Marc's wife and delivered the letter immediately to her. She read it,—and read it over and over again. But she didn't dare trust her eyes. She called her daughter, Anastasia, who had now grown into a charming young woman, and asked her to read the letter. Anastasia was even more surprised than her mother, for in the letter the following was clearly to be read:

*"Dear Wife,*

*As soon as you receive this letter you must marry my daughter Anastasia to the bearer immediately. If you do not obey these orders you will be severely punished, for you must realise that this youth is my best friend."*

The letter was signed with Marc's name, and in his own hand set with his own seal, so there could not be the slightest doubt as to what was his wish.

This was indeed like a bolt from the blue for the two young people. Anastasia looked at Vasilij, and had to admit that she could have been much worse off. Like all young women in those days she had no choice of her own anyway, and she had always feared her father would marry her to some old and ugly prince, or a tremendously rich and mean merchant. This was, at least, a kind and handsome young man.

Vasilij, however, had thought that when he had left the monastery, he was free to go out into the world and decide things for himself. No sooner was he free and ready to begin life, than it was arranged for him to marry a girl he had never seen before. Still, he looked at Anastasia and had to admit that she was beautiful, and when she smiled at him he found her so charming that he couldn't think there was a sweeter girl. If he had a chance to choose someone, he could certainly not have found anyone better. So the young people felt they had nothing to complain about and were quite happy.

The household of Marc the Rich became frantically busy. They had to prepare everything for the wedding. Vasilij had to get new fine clothes, and Anastasia had to have a wedding dress. But there were many hands to help them, and the following day everything was ready so that the wedding could take place according to Marc's orders.

A couple of months after the wedding there came a message that Marc was to return home from his journey. His wife, daughter and son-in-law went to the river port to meet him. When Marc came ashore and saw Vasilij standing there beside his beloved daughter, he flew into a passion. He took his wife aside and spoke to her. "What on earth is this? Haven't you carried out my orders?" was his outrageous outburst.

"But I have! Anastasia is married to Vasilij all right," she answered calmly.

"How dare you let such a thing happen!" he bellowed in a fury.

"But why? I dared not act otherwise. I just did as I was told," she said quietly. "You have written it yourself." With these words she went to fetch the letter and showed it to her angry husband.

Marc saw the letter and recognised his own handwriting and his seal. Everything seemed to be in perfect order except the meaning of the words. "How odd!" Marc thought. "But you shall not escape me, Vasilij! Three times have I tried to get rid of you, but now I am going to send you to a place where not even the ravens will find the remnants of your bones."

For about a month Vasilij lived quite happily with Marc as his father-in-law. Marc didn't show a sign of the hatred he felt for the young man. On the contrary, he was as kind to him as to his own daughter. No one would have noticed what he had in mind. But one day he called Vasilij and said to him:

"You know I have made you a warden of all my estates and treasuries. Now I've a very important task for you. Twelve years ago the Dragon-czar Zmy built a castle on a site belonging to me. I am going to send you to his country, which is far, far away, more than twelve kingdoms from here, and I want you to collect the rent which he owes me for all these years. Furthermore, I want you to ask him what has become of my twelve ships which have disappeared off his coasts during the last three years."

Vasilij did not dare to offer any objections and made the preparations for the long journey. He said goodbye to his wife, who had now become very dear to him, and set out on his long and dangerous trip.

He travelled on and on, sometimes on horseback, sometimes on foot, and at other times he had to sail down a river or across a sea. He saw many countries, large rivers and wide oceans, and everywhere he asked for the country of the Dragon-czar Zmy.

People he met only shook their heads saying they had never heard of such a strange monarch or czar, still less did they know anything about his country. "Dear young friend," they said to him, "If this Zmy is really a ruler of all dragons it sounds far too dangerous. Why not forget all about it, and not risk a visit to his country."

But Vasilij knew that if he ever wanted to go back home to his wife, he had to fulfil his task, and besides, he was looking forward to an adventure. So he travelled on, carefully counting the kingdoms he passed.

Quite a long time after he had passed the twelfth kingdom and was travelling across a wide field, he suddenly heard a strange voice saying "Where are you going, Vasilij the Unfortunate? Where is your journey's end?" Vasilij, astonished, looked round in all directions, but couldn't see anyone. Then he called out, "Who called me?—Answer!"

"It is I, the old and withered oak-tree," was the answer. "I ask you where you are going and whether your journey will be long."

Vasilij was astonished. "I am going to the Dragon-czar Zmy to collect his rent for the last twelve years."

"When you get there will you please remember me to Czar Zmy, and tell him that the old oak tree has been standing for more than five hundred years. It is now so rotten and withered that hardly any leaves are left on its aged branches. Ask him how long it still has to hold out in this world."

Vasilij listened attentively to the strange sighing words, and promised to bring the Dragon-czar the message. Then he continued his travels and came to a river. There was a ferry which was just leaving for the opposite bank, and Vasilij leaped on at the last minute. The old ferryman looked at him and said, "Have you a long journey ahead of you, Vasilij the Unfortunate?" And Vasilij answered, "I'm going to the Dragon-czar Zmy to collect the rent."

"If you come to Czar Zmy," said the ferryman, "will you please remember me to him, and tell him that I have now been ferrying people for more than thirty years, and I should like to know how long I will have to row to and fro across this river."

"Yes," said Vasilij, "I shall ask him."

He set out again, and before long he came to the sea. On the other side of a strait he saw a vast land, and he knew that at last he had come to the country of the Dragon-czar. This was how Marc the Rich had described it to him. The dragon's country was connected with the shore on which Vasilij stood in a peculiar way. For across the strait there lay a colossal whale stretched full length, so that it touched both shores. Along its back was a road on which people walked to and fro. Vasilij had only to follow the others and walk across. When he climbed up on the whale he heard it talking in a deep, human voice. "Where are you going, Vasilij the Unfortunate?" it asked. "Will your journey be long?"

"No," replied Vasilij, "at last I seem to have reached my goal. Isn't this the country of the Dragon-czar Zmy? I'm on an errand to him."

Again the whale spoke, "Yes, this is his country, and when you arrive at his palace, will you please give him a message from this poor whale who has been lying here stretched across the strait for two years with a road on his back? Tell him that riders and hikers are treading me almost down to my ribs. Neither by night nor by day do they give me any rest. Ask Zmy how long I still have to hold out."

"Yes," said Vasilij, "I promise to pass on your question."

He continued his walk for a while until he came to a large green field. In the middle stood a magnificent palace of white marble. Its roof was covered with mother-of-pearl shimmering with the colours of the rainbow, and the windows of crystal glittered like fire in the sunset.

The gate was open, so Vasilij had only to walk straight into the palace. He went from room to room, and was overwhelmed by their splendour. When he was living with Marc the Rich, he thought there couldn't be anything more splendid, but this was far beyond anything he thought possible. In the innermost room sat a Princess, more beautiful than anyone he had ever set eyes on.

"Oh! Is that you, Vasilij the Unfortunate, who has set foot in this dragon's nest?" she called out when she caught sight of him.

And Vasilij answered, "I've been sent here by Marc the Rich to collect the rent for twelve years that Czar Zmy owes him."

"Marc hasn't really sent you here for the rent, but to be

killed by the Dragon-czar. You are not the first one who has come here, but you are luckier than most of them. Czar Zmy isn't at home just now, or else it would have been the end for you like all the others who have been here in this terrible place. And now be off, as quick as ever you can! That's my advice."

"But I can't, the rent wasn't my only errand to Czar Zmy," said Vasilij. He then told the Princess all that had happened to him the latter part of his travels. Hardly had he finished his story when the whole place began to shake as if an earthquake was going to take place, and they heard a terrible rattling sound.

"That's Zmy!" exclaimed the terrified Princess and lifted the lid of a large chest that was in the room. "Quick, hide in here! And don't stir! Listen carefully to everything I'll say to Zmy."

They were only just in time. A terrible dragon came writhing into the room. Through some narrow cracks in the oak-chest Vasilij could see the horrible beast. His long scaly body filled most of the room, his head was like that of an enormous crocodile, and from his nostrils there came a shower of venom. When he opened his terrific mouth to speak he showed two rows of teeth, sharp as scissors.

"Oough, I say I'm tired! I've been travelling an immense way right through the widest country in the whole world from the Baltic to my own country, the Land of the Dragon beside the Japanese Sea." And then he opened his wide jaws into a dreadful yawn exposing all his terrible teeth and a throat like an abyss.

"I'm tired indeed. What I need is a nice long rest," said the beast coiling up to the Princess. Then he put his head in her lap and almost dropped off to sleep.

"Oh please, before you go to sleep, can't you listen to me for a moment? You never have time left for me. I want someone to talk to. You wise and clever Czar to whom nothing is concealed, without your help I shall never be able to interpret a curious dream I've had. I'm sure that you with your knowledge will be able to tell me its meaning before you go to sleep. You know when you are tired like this you can sleep for days and I shall have to sit here all by myself brooding upon my dream without a chance to solve it," said the Princess fawningly.

"Well then, let me hear it, but be quick!" commanded Zmy.

"I dreamt," began the Princess, "that I went into a wide field and there stood a lonely withered oak, and the oak spoke to me in the voice of a human. 'Ask Czar Zmy how long I shall stand here,' it said."

"It will stand there till a strong man gives it a hard kick with his foot. Then the whole oak will tumble down with its roots in the air. Under its roots I've hidden a treasure so great that not even Marc the Rich has as much," declared the dragon.

"But you clever Czar, I also dreamt that I came to a river where there was a ferry. The ferry-man asked me how long he still had to carry people to and fro across the river," continued the Princess.

"He has only himself to blame that he still sits there. He should let the next passenger using the ferry touch one of his oars and then jump ashore himself and push out the boat. Then he will be free and the other one will have to take his place as a ferryman for the rest of his life."

"Oh you wise Czar who can interpret all dreams," said the Princess, "in my dream I then came to a strait, and there as a bridge from one beach to the other lay a whale, who asked how long he had to endure the torment of people walking over his back to the other side."

"It just serves him right, he has to stay where he is until he

gives back the twelve ships belonging to Marc the Rich that
he has swallowed up during the course of the last three years.
After that he may be free to go out to sea again and have a
rest." Zmy now turned over on his other side and before long
the whole palace echoed with his loud and heavy snoring, the
crystal windows shivered and the marble walls shook.

The charming Princess rose from her seat and went to the
chest, lifted the lid, and without saying a word she let Vasilij
out. Vasilij wanted to thank his beautiful rescuer, but she made
a sign to warn him from saying anything. Vasilij knew everything he needed for carrying out his task and hastened away
as quickly as he could.

He didn't rest until he came to the strait where the whale
lay. As soon as the whale caught sight of him, he asked him at
once, "Have you been to the Czar? Did he give you any
message for me?"

"Let me first pass over to the other side, and I'll tell you,"
answered Vasilij, and walked over on the back of the whale
till he stood safely on the other beach. Then he said, "If you
can give back the twelve ships belonging to Marc the Rich
which you swallowed three years ago, you will be released
from your torment."

The whale cleared his throat, opened his wide jaws, coughed
a little—and out came a ship. Once again he coughed and
there came another ship. He did this again and again until
twelve fine ships were floating on the water, quite undamaged,
with their crews and everything else in perfect order. They had
only to sail to Marc the Rich.

The whale beat the water with his big tail and made a sudden
turn, so that the water splashed high up on land, and Vasilij
had to hurry away as fast as he could to avoid being drowned.

Soon he came to the ferry. "Oh Vasilij the Unfortunate,

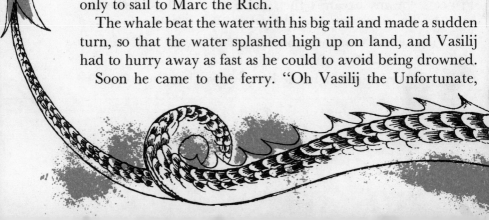

have you spoken to Czar Zmy about me? What did he say?" asked the ferryman.

"As soon as you have ferried me over to the other side, I will tell you," answered Vasilij. When Vasilij was on the other shore, he said, "The first person who comes here after me, you should ask to touch the oars, then jump ashore yourself, and push the boat out into the river. The other person will have to take your place and you will be free."

At last Vasilij came to the withered oak. He went up to it and with all his force he gave it a kick. The huge old oak fell to the ground with a terrible crash, its roots in the air, and there underneath were uncountable treasures, heaps of silver, gold and jewels.

Vasilij looked round. He didn't know what to do with all these goods. He couldn't carry them alone. But when he looked towards the sea, he saw twelve ships sailing along. He recognized Marc's ships and in the stern of the first one he saw the three venerable old men he had met once before.

"We greet thee, Vasilij the *Fortunate,* and may that now be thy name," said the three old men, and went ashore.

The crew on the twelve ships greeted Vasilij as their rescuer and master. They helped him to load all the treasures on board the ships. Very pleased, Vasilij now returned to Marc's home with the lost ships and far more money and gold and silver than Marc had ever claimed.

Anastasia, who thought Vasilij lost for ever, was delighted at his return. Marc the Rich, however, was highly disappointed. "However could it happen that anyone could have escaped the terrible Dragon-czar?" he thought. "It wasn't the twelve ships I wanted, not even the treasures. I wanted this young man dead."

He had to talk to the Dragon-czar himself about the matter

and as soon as possible. He ordered his most swift-footed horse to be put to his best coach, then he set off at once to consult with Zmy how he could best get rid of his troublesome godson.

It was a long journey, but at last he came to the river and saw the ferryman who was to take him across. He was in such a hurry that when he jumped on board, the boat rocked heavily under his feet. He had to clasp something so as not to fall into the water. The ferryman quickly held out the oars for him to seize, and then jumped ashore and pushed the boat out into the river. This left Marc doomed to be the new ferryman for the river, and he may be doing it still.

Vasilij the Fortunate became the owner of Marc's whole fortune. But he never turned a beggar away from his gate, and gladly shared his wealth with his poorer friends. In Marc's magnificent house he lived with his wife, the lovely Anastasia, happily ever after.

# The Two Humpbacked Fiddlers
*A story from Germany*

FRIEDEL was the merriest person in the whole town. In spite of the ugly hump on his back he was always ready with a smile and a joke, and when he played his fiddle everyone listened to his gay tunes. Even the busy ants stopped to listen on their way to the nest as they dragged their straws along, and old Peter in the poor-house forgot his gout, and beat time with the only leg he was able to move. The children in the town clapped their hands as soon as they saw a glimpse of his fair curly hair.

"Friedel is here! Friedel is here!" they shouted and hurried away to the large field outside the town walls. There they danced spellbound until they were out of breath and out of their shoes, and Friedel's fingers were so tired that he could not play the strings any more.

Then they threw coins in his ragged cap, and he thanked them with that gay smile of his and went away singing.

It was quite a long walk from the large field to his home. First he had to pass a wood, then walk through the old town with all its narrow streets and alleys, before he reached the little cottage with the thatched roof at the south gate of the town wall. But when he came home tired and hungry his mother sat under the cherry-tree nodding at him, her wrinkled face beaming with contentment. Then Friedel felt happy, for he knew his mother was as proud of him as if he were a prince. She sat happily watching him munching rye bread and drinking his soup, while she listened to all his news and tales of his day's work. Sometimes he had only a few coins in his pocket when he came home; other days he had a little more. But however little it was, Friedel and his mother were just as pleased when they went to bed, and no prince on his bed of eiderdown could sleep more satisfied than poor Friedel on his bed of straw. And yet he had a deformity that could have made many a happy man sad. His handsome, friendly face sat deep down between his shoulders and his back was twisted into a hump. But he bore his misfortune as gallantly and bravely as he carried his fiddle, so that everyone had long ago stopped thinking about it. Hump-backed or not, they still felt that Friedel was the nicest boy on earth.

To be content with a little was something he had inherited from his mother. No one had ever heard her complaining that life was hard and full of troubles. If the turnips were rotten one year, she consoled herself with the cabbage. If her feet were frostbitten so that she was unable to move them for many months, she thanked the good Lord that she could still use her fingers to knit socks. And when the neighbours said how sorry they were that Friedel had a humpback, she answered with a broad smile, "Well, well, can anybody tell me if there is anything really wrong with that boy? If he has a hump on his back it must be useful for something." And that was what Friedel himself thought.

In the same town lived another hunchback, Heinz, who also played the fiddle. Yet he was completely different from Friedel, he was as miserable as Friedel was gay. Friedel loved his fiddle and played it for the trees and flowers, for dogs and cats, for people old and young, for whoever could enjoy it. He played just for the joy of being alive.

Heinz, on the other hand, never played for joy, but only because it was the best way a poor hunchback could earn his living. His brown eyes never lit up with enthusiasm when he drew the bow over his violin as Friedel's did. He simply played a tune for people to dance, but they never danced with the same delight as they did to Friedel's music.

There was just one feeling that they both shared: their belief that the Burgomaster's daughter, little Ilse Elbegardt, was the prettiest maiden they had ever seen. On Sundays when she sat beside her stern father in their carved, high bench in church, the sun shining through the coloured window panes on her rosy face and long fair plaits bound like a shimmering crown round her head, then Friedel with the best will in the world could not concentrate on the sermon, and Heinz's bitter eyes stared at the girl as if she were an angel. But in his heart he grew still more bitter and angry with his deformity, in complete contrast to Friedel, who just thought to himself how lucky he was to be able to see and admire her beauty.

One morning while he was thinking about the Burgomaster's daughter, singing merrily to himself, he met miserable Heinz. "How can you be happy and gay, you silly fool?" asked Heinz sullenly. "I can't see that either of us has much to be gay about."

"Why not? I'm thinking of Ilse Elbegardt, and you could be happy for less."

"I am thinking of her too," answered Heinz, "but the more I think of her, the more downhearted I feel. A girl like that will always be too good for a poor, deformed wretch like me. Why is one man born poor and ugly and not another? Why have you and I got a hump on our backs and Ilse Elbegardt has all the happiness and good fortune in the world? Can you explain that?"

"Well, tell me first, do you grudge her that?" smiled Friedel. "Why are there not only butterflies and birds in their world, but also worms and frogs? Why doesn't a dragonfly carry straws like the ants? And after all who can tell if one day you or I might not marry Ilse Elbegardt? A hump is of course a hump and not exactly very attractive, but God is God and nobody knows what his intention was in giving them to us. So cheer up." And with that Friedel went away.

It was a lovely summer evening. The sun was just setting and its last rays shone over the vine-covered hills. Somehow Friedel completely forgot that it would soon be dark until he found himself standing in the wood which was now become pitch black so that he could not even see his own hand.

"God bless me, this is a bit uncanny!" he thought to himself, a little frightened. He tried to find his way out of the wood, but this was easier said than done. He groped about, but everywhere he got tangled up in trees or bushes or stumbled over stones and tussocks. The owls stared at him with eyes that were sharp and shiny in the dark, fluttering their wings. The bats touched his cheek or his white shirt, and the small fireflies whirled through the air like sparks. It was really eerie, and a boy less brave than Friedel would probably have been scared to death. He did not give up easily, and at last the moon came out from behind the clouds and shone a bright and silvery path right in front of his feet. He had walked round in circles and was in the same place as when he started. Friedel burst out laughing to see how stupid he was without any light to help him.

"Thank you, you are a regular trump!" he cried up to the moon with a friendly nod. "I shall play you a beautiful tune, if you care to listen."

Then he put the violin to his chin and played while he was walking along, followed by dancing fairies swinging around him in a veil of light over the grass.

As he reached the other side of the town gate, the clock in the church tower struck twelve deep, solemn strokes. Friedel thought that the chiming sounded unusually strange tonight, and he could not help feeling a bit uneasy again. The shadows fell so long and fearfully from the old church tower and the gables of the tall houses, and the cries of the night birds echoed through the still air. Friedel began to think he could see faint fire-flames passing through the air.

Suddenly he though he saw some misty figures flying above the roofs of the houses. But at a second glace he decided it must be a storm brewing and the clouds scudding across the sky. He stopped to listen to a strange song and then decided it must have been the sighing of the wind. Finally he reached the large fish market. But here he stopped, paralysed in amazement, and almost dropped his precious fiddle.

The whole market was lit up as if for a magnificent feast, not by lanterns or torches but by moving flames flickering and shimmering, now blood-red, now yellow, and then sparkling blue. Thousands and thousands of female creatures crowded around each other and the crowd increased every minute. Amazed and scared though Friedel was, his curiosity made him draw nearer to discover what was going on.

It suddenly occurred to him that tonight must be a witches' Sabbath. In all countries there were four great feasts a year and it was said that on these nights the witches gathered in the fish markets for their celebrations. Friedel had never quite believed in it, because when he saw the mild eyes of his mother, he could not accept that there was anything as bad and wicked as witches in this world.

Now, however, he saw them with his own eyes, and had to admit he was mistaken. Well, they could have been uglier, and they carried themselves proudly in their dresses of silk and velvet. Some of them were quite pretty to look at, as long as they did not turn round to show their queer hollow backs.

They caught sight of Friedel, and at once he was surrounded by a crowd of witches. "A fiddle, a fiddler, that's just what we need," they shouted with joy.

They took Friedel by the hand and led him up to a table groaning under the weight of delicacies piled on it. There was the finest salmon he could ever imagine, sparkling golden wine and a variety of sausages and sauerkraut so invitingly hot that he could not resist saying, "Oh, what a treat!" because hunger was gnawing inside him, and he felt like an empty sack.

"Well, help yourself!" said a splendid lady with a heavy golden chain round her neck, "and may it do you good."

"Thank you, it certainly will," answered Friedel. Never in his life had he eaten so much and felt as satisfied as he now did.

"Don't you want another helping, my dear boy?" asked the witch, when he rose from the table. "Oh, no, I'm sure I've had enough for a whole week. Isn't there some way I could repay your kindness?"

"Yes, an excellent way. You are a fiddler, and we like to dance."

"All right," Friedel answered readily. He jumped up on a bench and put the fiddle to his chin.

The witches stood in a circle round Friedel while he watched them for a minute and found they looked so severe and sad, that he felt sorry for them.

"I'll try to liven them up a bit," he thought, and then he smiled at them. He played the merriest melodies he could think of with such a lilting rhythm that, almost unconsciously, heads were set wagging and feet dancing in time to the music. They were a little hesitant at first but then their faces cleared and they began to smile first with one corner of their mouth then with the other as the dance became faster and faster. Never had Friedel played like tonight. His fiddle sparkled with life and laughter as he swept his bow over the strings, the witches whirled about on their broom sticks and their hair flew right up into the air, the golden chain on the splendid lady rocked up

and down like a nut-shell on the waves. Friedel stared at them in delight and wonder and their wild grace enchanted him. But in the end he grew very dizzy, his fingers went numb, and he sank exhausted onto the bench.

Then the lady with the golden chain went up to him.

"Friedel," she said, "you are a marvellous fiddler. You don't only play with your fingers but also with your heart, and we owe you a lot of thanks." Saying this she put her left hand on his hump, murmured some magic words and Friedel felt his hump disappear. The witch put it into an empty box which she closed immediately.

Just then the clock in the tower boomed one dull stroke. In a flash the whole market was emptied. The host of witches flew away on their broomsticks like a gigantic black cloud. The richly laden table sank down into the earth, and the flames flickered and went out. Friedel stood alone in the moonlight by the well in the middle of the empty fish market, wondering if it had all been a dream or only a vision.

"In any case, one thing is certain, I feel sleepy, terribly sleepy," he murmured and he hurried home as fast as he could, and fell on to his hard bed, fully dressed, and fell asleep immediately.

He didn't get up with the sun next morning as usual. The cock was already in the middle of his fifth cock-a-doodle-do before he woke and rubbed his eyes. Just then his mother came in with a cup of milk and a piece of bread for his breakfast.

"Lazy bones," she began, but one glance at him made her drop the cup in amazement.

"Friedel, Friedel, what on earth has happened to you?" she cried in alarm.

"What?" Friedel said. "I have overslept, which could happen to anybody."

"Oh, it's not that, but where is your hump? And where have you got these fine clothes from? She clasped her hands, simply thunderstruck.

"My hump?" Friedel felt at his back. Yes indeed, it was gone. His clothes? He looked down at his legs, they were clothed in a pair of silk sockings as fine as those of a nobleman, and light brown leather shoes with fine silver buckles that he had never seen before, nor the green velvet jacket.

"Look, Mother! I've become a real prince!" And he gave a wild dance of joy, whirling her round till she lost her breath and collapsed.

"Well, my dear child," panted his mother, "however did this happen? You haven't done something wrong have you?"

"You don't really believe that, do you?" Friedel said looking right into her eyes with his honest look. "No, Mother, you have brought me up too well for that. But I've played merry tunes for witches, that's what I've done. Why shouldn't they have a jolly swing round like everyone else? But I never dreamt I'd be so generously rewarded." Friedel put his hands gaily into the pockets of his new trousers. His fingers touched some small hard objects. Puzzled, he seized hold of them and pulled out a handful of golden coins. He put his hands into his pockets again, and again he got his hands full of coins. No matter how often he repeated this, the same thing happened every time.

Finally, their little wooden table was piled so high with golden coins that it could not carry any more, and the sun itself looked in through the low window to find out what was glittering so brilliantly in competition with its own golden rays.

"For goodness' sake, don't bring out any more!" cried Friedel's mother, who in her amazement had sunk down on the only chair in the room. "What on earth shall we do with all that money?"

It was the first time in her life that the old woman had felt worried.

"Well, Mother, there are always plenty of poor people to give it to," Friedel said. "And you need a little more comfort in your old age too. I've often thought about that, but I've never been able to do anything about it before. Now we can dance to quite a different tune!"

Once again he whirled round with the old woman so fast that she lost her wooden shoes.

"Now, Mother dear, we shall have a real treat!" And he hurried out swinging his cap. When he returned he had a big

93

goose under one arm and a couple of bottles of golden wine under the other. For the first time that poor cottage was filled with the smell of sweet wine and roast goose as good as any that came from the richest kitchens in the world.

"Bother," Friedel said, "We have no glasses. But it doesn't matter, even if it is the first time anybody has drunk fine old Rhine wine out of pottery mugs. One thing we must promise one another, Mother dear, to be as content in our wealth as we were in our poverty."

"Yes, my boy, we shall," answered the old woman. And the best thing was, they kept their promise.

The first thing Friedel did, when he had got used to being a wealthy man, was to buy a nice house with a steep gable and a funny door-knocker on it. His mother thought that the queen herself could not live any better when she went about in her rooms with their high windows and finely carved cupboards filled with delicacies, or when she sat in her soft armchair by the window looking out between her flower pots down to the square where her Friedel, in such a wonderful way, had found his fortune.

One day Friedel took the Burgomaster's daughter by the hand and walked firmly with her up the broad steps to the town hall, right into the severe Burgomaster's room where he sat in his office chair, looking very wise and powerful, as a burgomaster should. Really he was a good-natured man and not exceptionally wise.

"What has brought you here, you fiddler?" he asked Friedel.

"Most humbly I would ask Your Honour to give me your daughter's hand in marriage," answered Friedel.

"Is that all?" began the Burgomaster with a smile, but then added more severely, "What can you offer her?"

"My heart, to begin with," said Friedel.

"What silly nonsense. Have you nothing else to offer?"

"Well, this," Friedel answered, grabbling in his pocket, and he began piling up golden coins on the table, until the eyes of the Burgomaster shone like the pile of coins.

"Yes, take her, take her, go ahead," he panted, enchanted.

So Friedel and Ilse Elbegardt became husband and wife, and their wedding was celebrated with great merriment and fun. Friedel bought a new house beside the old one, so that he and his wife lived right next to his mother. He and Ilse were the happiest young couple you could see, and his old mother was happy too.

But there was one person in the town who was far from happy, Heinz. As he played his fiddle at Friedel's wedding, he was twisted with jealousy. He had always been envious of Friedel for his brave spirit, but now that he stood as tall and straight as any man, he really hated him. His lips trembled with envy and rage as he tried to drink to the health of the bride and bridegroom.

"Don't look so sad, Heinz," Friedel said full of kindness. "Why, you could make your fortune as well as I could."

"I'm born to misfortune," Heinz muttered unhappily.

"No man can say that while he still has his life ahead of him. Why not go out in the fish market on the next witches' Sabbath night, that's my advice," urged Friedel.

These words echoed in the ears of Heinz. Once again the witches' Sabbath night came round. But this time it was no longer summer, it was Hallow'een, late in the autumn. Dark clouds swept over the town on this stormy night like big black birds of prey, the owls screamed and the wind whistled. But Heinz did not care. With his fiddle under his arm and his cloak flapping over his hump he hurried as fast as he could to the fish market. He was there even before the clock struck twelve, trembling with expectations and impatience as he looked out over the vast empty square. It was as quiet as usual. The houses with their pointed gables, old stone figures, and leaded panes stood there in silence sleeping in the night like their inhabitants. Only the weathercock on Friedel's house squeaked in the wind, and Heinz thought it sounded like scornful laughter because he had been deceived into coming out on this stormy night.

"If you have fooled me, and mocked me in my misfortune, I mean to have my revenge!" he hissed shaking his fist threateningly at Friedel's window.

Then he sat on the edge of the old stone wall, indignant and angry. The church clock struck twelve. At that moment the air was filled with the beating of a thousand wings, and the whole square was lit up by a dazzling light. By a stroke of magic the market-place was crowded with female creatures. The long tables were again splendidly laid with glittering bowls and dishes filled with delicacies of all kinds, while coloured flames went flashing through the air. The lady with the magnificent golden chain went up to Heinz as she had before gone to Freidel.

"You are a fiddler, aren't you?" she asked pointing to his violin, with her hand adorned with rings. "Won't you strike up a dance for us?"

"Nobody ever asks what a wretch of a fellow like me wants," answered Heinz sullenly with a suspicious look. "Whatever rabble I play to I expect to be handsomely paid."

"I can't say you are especially amiable," the lady with the golden chain answered. "We pay according to what you deserve. But before you play, you may help yourself to anything on the tables."

There was no need to repeat this twice to Heinz. As greedy as a shark he flung himself upon the food and ate until he was almost sick. On top of it all, he filled his pockets with as much as he could lay hands on, so that he looked as if his body had humps all over.

"Perhaps you won't mind playing now?" the lady with the golden chain asked coldly.

Heinz put the violin under his chin and began playing indifferently and sullenly, as was his custom. He made even less attempt to please than usual for he thought he knew what kind of audience he had before him. This host of witches ought to be grateful that an honest man bothered to even come and play for them. How he played and what he played did not matter, so his playing grew more and more careless. Finally he neither cared about rhythm nor tune, as if an evil spirit had got hold of his bow. It swung in his hand, and the tunes grew wilder and wilder, shriller and more furious. The witches whirled about as if they were taking part in a senseless race. It was impossible to keep time and their threatening glances were anything but friendly. A furious murmur reached his ears, and fists were shaken at him, and when he at last dropped his bow in exhaustion and sank down on the bench, the lady with the golden chain came up to him with a severe look.

"Fall on your knees, and receive your reward!" ordered the lady. In her hand she held a closed box which Heinz watched greedily.

"Is that my reward?" he asked eagerly.

"Yes, the reward you *deserve*," replied the lady with a significant stress on the last word, and the crowd around them laughed mockingly.

"I demand to be honestly paid!" cried Heinz excited. "That box may contain a lot, but Friedel got more than that. You can at least give me that golden cup." Heinz stretched out his hand to grasp the most precious thing on the table. The lady lifted her hand, and gave him a box on the ear, so hard and burningly painful that he dropped the cup at once and sank down on his knees. Once again the witches laughed, and before he knew how it happened, the lady took the little box with Friedel's hump out of her pocket and fixed it on his back beside the one he already had.

"That is what you deserve for your carelessness," she said. "Perhaps from this time onwards you will remember your duties whether you work for men or witches."

Suddenly one strong, dull stroke boomed from the church tower, everything disappeared like a vision and the storm howled round the corners of the vast empty square. Stunned as if it had all been an evil dream, poor Heinz hurried home to his miserable hovel where he soon fell asleep.

He woke up after a heavy sleep, when the sun was already high up in the sky. The first thing he did was to see if his hump was gone. But alas, to his great horror, he discovered that instead of one hump he now had two on his back, like a camel.

But his pockets felt heavy: perhaps there was gold in them. He grasped eagerly at what was inside and pulled out a handful of gravel.

Desperately he fell down again on his straw bed and burst out crying. He now vented his passion on Friedel. Who had deluded him into this venture and brought him double misfortune, if not Friedel? Now he should suffer for it! And he rushed like a madman to Friedel's house.

Friedel was sitting on the bench outside his house in the sunshine, happily playing his fiddle, when Heinz, pale and desperate, rushed across to him, pouring abuse at him, as he related the events of the night.

"You evil-hearted wretch. You wanted to make me still more unhappy and miserable than I already was. It was you who advised me, you scoundrel," he cried angrily.

Friedel listened horrified. He felt too sorry for Heinz to mind his outburst of fury. With eyes full of tears, he said mildly, "I never meant to do you any harm. On the contrary, I thought the same would happen to you as happened to me. It's not my fault that you didn't please the witches. I am very sorry for you and share your trouble as if you were my brother. I know what it means to be a cripple although I am no longer one myself. From now on you shall be as a brother to me. You need never be lonely again, as my home will be your home too, Ilse will be as a sister to you, and my old mother certainly has a heart large enough for all of us. Perhaps between us we can help you to forget your bad luck. You will do this with us won't you?" And he reached out his hand.

Heinz stood for a moment stiff and dumb without grasping Friedel's hand. When Ilse also came and looked at him saying, "Please accept Friedel's offer, Heinz!" it was as if something hard in his heart had given way. Never before had anyone been so kind to him. He blushed in shyness for he hardly knew what it meant to be anything but grumpy.

"Thank you, Friedel," he answered and shook his hand. From that day Heinz stayed in Friedel's house, as an old friend, and many years later when Ilse and Friedel's children grew up they had no better friend and playmate than dear old uncle Heinz.

# The Tale of the Three Lemons
## A story from France, based on that of de Laboulaye

ONCE UPON A TIME there lived a King who was the last of an old dynasty. He and his Queen prayed for a son for many years, and, when at last their wish came true and a little Prince was born, he became dearer to them than anything in the world.

The King was anxious that his son should be taught every accomplishment that was fitting for a noble Prince, so the young Carlino grew up able to swing a sword more skilfully, and ride a horse more gracefully, than any other in his father's country. He also loved daring adventures: challenging danger by sailing his small boat on a rough sea, while his old father sat anxiously at home waiting for his return. The King often rebuked his son, and said, "Remember, you are the comfort of my old age and my hope for the future." But secretly the old King admired the courage of his son.

In one thing only was Carlino a disappointment to his father. While other young knights at the court tried to win the favours of the beautiful ladies, Carlino was shy in their presence and avoided their company. Almost every day the old King pressed upon his son the urgency of choosing a wife.

"I can't end my days in peace before I see you married and I know that my grandchildren will make our family secure," he often said.

But Carlino had nothing to answer. He set out as before on his keen adventures.

One day when the King and his son sat at dinner eating their dessert, the old King rebuked the Prince as usual for not yet having chosen a bride. Carlino had a plate with cream in front of him, and was just slicing a piece of a fruit to eat with it, when he cut his finger. A few drops of blood fell on to the cream. While the Prince watched the crimson blood spreading over the white cream a strange idea flashed into his mind and he cried out:

"Look father, how beautiful these two colours are. If I ever marry, it must be a girl with skin as pale as this cream and lips as red as this blood. Somewhere on this earth there lives a girl like this, and however far off she may be I shall find her, even if I have to seek her at the end of the world."

His words came like a heavy blow to his father.

"My dear son, you cannot mean to leave me here alone? I may never see you again!" he called out in agony. "Have you completely lost your senses! You who are the only one to uphold our family, and the successor to my throne. Banish these wild ideas from your mind at once."

"Father, you have always urged me to find a bride and now when I show my willingness to obey you say you don't like it," cried Carlino, quite disappointed.

"Are there not plenty of young ladies of high rank in my kingdom, and fair Princesses in the neighbouring countries that would suit you? Is it really necessary to set out on dangerous adventures from which you may never return? Remember also that I am now an old man and may no longer be alive if, in spite of everything, one day you return."

But once he had made up his mind, nothing could make Carlino change it, and the old King was forced to give way to his son's wish to set out on his travels across the world, though in his heart he was convinced he would never see his son again.

Setting out gaily, Carlino started his search through every town, village, and castle. Everywhere, he looked at the young girls and noble ladies, but nowhere did he find the one he had dreamed of. At last he arrived at the port of Marseilles and decided to take a boat from there to sail away to other continents.

As he stood on board the ship, he felt for the first time that he had started on a real adventure. Nothing could stop him, neither the storms of the sea, nor the heat of the desert wind. He overcame everything and withstood every hardship in the hope that he would at last find the lady he sought.

He travelled on and ever on, south and east through strange countries where no travellers had ventured before. He saw more girls than he could count, but not one was the bride he was seeking.

At last he had travelled so far that he had come to the end of the world. He stood on a desolate shore with bare cliffs reaching out to a sea that had no end. There was no sign of a boat nor of any life at all—only the sea and the sky stretching out until they met, far out on the horizon.

Carlino was very disappointed. Had he travelled so far and resisted so many dangers for nothing? Was there really nothing else to do but to return home again without having seen the bride he had vowed he would find?

He wandered across the rocks and the cliffs, feeling sad and bitter. To his astonishment he almost tripped over an old man, lying on the far side of a cliff. The man lay outstretched on the cliff as if to let the sun warm up his old and shrivelled limbs.

"Good evening, father," the Prince said gently. "Can you tell me if there is any land beyond this vast sea?"

"No, my son," the old man replied. "No land has ever been found on the other side of this water, and those who have tried to find out have never returned. When I was a child, they used to say that far out there, where no human had ever been, was the Island of Destiny. But that is only a story."

"If I could get hold of a boat I should like to find out for myself," Carlino declared.

"If it's just a boat you want, you will find one in a little creek behind these rocks," said the old man pointing to some bare rocks behind them. "I used to be a fisherman in my younger days, but that is now a long time ago. The old vessel won't be in a very good state."

"Never mind," cried Carlino glad at the opportunity of continuing his adventure. "I'll take the boat and try to find out what lies beyond this sea."

"Goodbye, my son! And don't forget I've warned you!" were the last words the Prince heard from the old man, as he boarded the little boat and hoisted the sails to set off.

Luckily the kind old man had supplied him with food for several days, for he sailed for more than a week without seeing anything but water around him. Carlino soon gave up counting the days. The weather was fine, with a stiff breeze; and the little boat rode the waves better than he had expected.

One day when the wind had dropped, Carlino noticed to his surprise that the little boat sailed on as fast as ever. "There must be some magic in this," he thought. "The sea is quite calm and the sails are slack, yet the boat is flying ahead on the water."

Fear crept into his heart as he wondered what lay ahead.

The boat sped across the waves from early morning till late afternoon. Then in the distance Carlino saw a dark cliff rising out of the waves. To his horror the little boat sailed towards it as swiftly as ever. With a groan of despair, Carlino prepared for certain death, but the moment he felt the boat being torn to pieces on the rocks he saw a ledge in the cliff and with one desperate jump managed to gain a hold.

It was no easy matter climbing the rocky cliff, and he was forced to crawl up on his hands and knees, tearing his skin and clothes on the sharp rocks.

At last he reached the top, to be greeted by a desolate scene of snow, ice and rocks. Not a blade of grass or a bush was in sight. He looked again and noticed hidden in the rocks a tiny tumbledown cottage with a roof covered with stones. "Just the place for a rest," he thought to himself as he went up to it.

He knocked at the door—no answer. Pushing it slowly open he peeped inside. The little room was bare save for a large loom, placed right in the centre. And from this loom welled a tapestry so large that it filled not just the wall, but almost the whole room. It seemed to have no beginning and no end. Its pattern was stranger than anything the Prince had ever seen. It was crowded with people young and old, large and small, of every country and every situation. Merchants and beggars jostled in the towns, peasants toiled in the fields and kings and knights sat in palaces and castles. Around them were forests, hills and deserts full of wild beasts and small friendly animals.

Over the loom sat an old, old woman with a gigantic pair of scissors in her hand. She looked like death itself, a bundle of bones covered with a shrivelled brown skin, and cunning eyes set back in deep hollows.

Now and then she jumped from her seat and with her big

scissors made a cut in the weaving—anywhere she felt like, it seemed to Carlino.

Everytime she cut a figure out, a wail of sorrow was heard, and the groans and gasps of a dying person. Carlino shivered where he stood in the doorway. But these sounds seemed not to disturb the old woman in the least, she only smiled complacently, and sat quietly down again mending the hole.

When the Prince opened the door a ray of light streamed into the room and fell on the weaving. In this ray of light the old woman discovered the dark shadow of a human being. Without turning her head she called out in a hoarse voice: "You wretched man, save yourself while there still is time! Do not put your foot within this door, or you will no longer be one of the living. I know who you are and why you have come. But I can't do anything for you. Try instead to find my sister: she is Life but I am Death."

Carlino at once shut the door and fled from the fateful cottage. Fear had driven away his weariness. Hardly looking where he ran he climbed the nearest hill, and rushed down the other side. He stopped panting for breath and looked around him. The countryside had changed completely. He stood in a beautiful valley. Rich, high cornfields and green orchards lay around him. Under a tree he saw a blind woman busily spinning, surrounded by several different spinning-wheels. On each wheel she spun a different thread: gold, silver, flax, hemp, wool and silk. The woman moved from one spinning-wheel to the other and spun a little on each.

Carlino greeted her and was just going to tell her about his travels, when she interrupted him saying, "You may as well save your story for my youngest sister, my dear. I wish I could do something for you, but alas, I am blind. I hardly know what I'm doing myself. I just touch the first spinning-wheel I can reach and spin a little on it. Wealth or poverty, success or failure, happiness or misery, all depend on these threads. Whatever I spin by chance decides the fate of a new born baby.

"So you see there is little I can do of my own free will. Though I am the Fairy of Life, I am also the Slave of Fate. But my youngest sister the Fairy of Birth may perhaps be able to help you."

Carlino rested a while in the orchard, and refreshed himself with some fruit, to give himself new strength and a lighter heart to continue his quest. It was not long before he found the last one of the three fairies. In a lovely garden he saw a young woman, beautiful as Spring itself. The green grass sparkled with tiny new flowers, and every tree and bush was in bud. The fruit trees were in full blossom, a hen scuttled about her newly-hatched chickens, and new-born lambs played round their mothers. Everywhere Carlino saw the first smiling moments of life.

The lovely fairy greeted the Prince with a friendly smile, and said, "Never before has a human being set foot on this island. With your courage and skill you are most welcome, my friend. Your long and adventurous journey has come to an end, for it is in my power to give you what you have set out to find. But first you must have a good meal and a long rest."

When he had eaten the delicious food she put before him and rested under the sweet-smelling blossoms, Carlino asked the kind fairy if he could now meet the girl who was to be his bride.

"No, my dear Carlino," the fairy answered. "You will have to wait till you get home. I have no girl for you here, but it is in my power to help you find the one you wish." With these words the fairy handed Carlino three lemons and a little knife with a silver blade and a handle of mother-of-pearl.

"Take these," she said. "When you have returned to your country cut one of the lemons in half with the knife. But you must be careful to do this near a well, so that you have some water at hand. From the lemon will come a girl like the one in your dreams. She will ask you to give her something to drink, and you must obey at once for *if you don't give her a glass of water she will disappear,* and you will never see her again. I have given you three lemons so that if you fail with the first two you must succeed with the third, or you will lose everything."

The Prince thanked the fairy for her precious gift, and promised to remember what she had told him.

"You will find a boat in the bay on the other side of my garden," she told him. "It is my own ship and it will take you back to your country. Just leave it on the shore when you have reached home, and it will return to this bay. And now, good luck to you and farewell."

The end of the world is a long, long way and even though the Prince had a fine boat that sailed him right to the coast of his own country, it took several weeks to make the trip. At last he landed on the shore of his own country not far from his father's castle.

The fairy's boat turned and sailed away again as soon as Carlino had jumped ashore and by the time he had climbed up the beach it had vanished in the distance. He set out at once to find a well for he decided that he could not return home without the girl he had sought across the world. He came to a little village clustered near a grove of trees. In the middle of the grove Carlino found a well, and deep inside he saw the sparkle of fresh water. He sat down quite close to the well and filled a glass with water. Then he took from his pocket the three lemons and the little knife that he had been given on the Island of Destiny. He cut the first lemon in half. Out came a tiny girl

of such exquisite beauty that Carlino had never seen any to compare with her in all his travels. She grew and grew until she stood before him: a perfect young girl. Then she said in a soft voice: "Will you give me something to drink?"

Carlino was so entranced by her that he could neither move nor speak. She was so like the girl he had seen in his dreams that forgetting everything else, he sat in dreamy admiration of her beauty. Alas, in a few minutes the whole vision was gone.

"What a fool I am!" he cried out in desperation. "What a stupid idiot, not to do as I was told!"

He cheered up a little when he remembered he still had two lemons left. So he took the second one and cut it in half. Again a tiny young girl stepped out, and when she had grown to a normal size Carlino found her even more beautiful than the first one. When she said:

"Will you give me something to drink?" he didn't even hear her for again he had drifted into a trance as he looked at her face. This girl was lovelier than the first, but alas, even less permanent—within seconds of making her request she had vanished.

The disappointment was so great that Carlino burst into tears.

"What a fool I am! A useless good-for-nothing. For the second time I've let my happiness slip through my fingers."

His grief was so great that he forgot everything. It was some time before he remembered that he still had one lemon left. This time he vowed to himself that he would not give the fairy a single glance before he gave her a glass of water, and he would hold it ready in his hand.

He cut the last lemon and seized the glass at once, not looking up until he heard a sweet voice saying,

"Will you give me something to drink?"

At once Carlino handed the young woman in front of him the glass. Only then did he dare to look up, and what he saw filled his heart with great joy. Now he did not regret that he had lost his first two dreams. This girl had the beauty of both sun and moon, spring and summer! She was enchantment and happiness itself. She smiled at him with dark blue eyes, like the evening summer sky, and with red lips, redder than a red rose, while her golden hair floated in the breeze like sunbeams.

Again Carlino gazed in wonder, but this time his dream did not disappear. At last he managed to speak:

"I've journeyed to the end of the world to find you, facing every peril, every adventure. I've even dared to visit the Island of Destiny for your sake. Whoever you are, it is you I have dreamed of all the time. Will you make my dream end happily and be my wife?"

"Yes, I know what you have endured to find me, and that is why I have come from the land of the fairies," she answered smiling. Then she went up to him and put her hand into his and promised to become his wife.

Joyfully they set out to the King's castle. The old King hugged Carlino with tears streaming down his cheeks, for he had despaired of ever seeing his beloved son again. And the King, the Queen and the whole court loved Carlino's dream-bride so that the wedding feast was the happiest in the kingdom.

# Ljungby Horn and Pipe
## A story from Sweden

HUNDREDS OF YEARS AGO the Lady Ulfstand, mistress and owner of Ljungby castle, sat in her large hall. She was very distressed. Once again there had been a fierce quarrel with her daughter, who, ignoring her gentle mother's attempts to quieten her, had flown into a rage over nothing, stamping her feet, her dark eyes flashing in fury; the hall still held the echoes of the cruel, spiteful words she had screamed at her mother as she rushed out, slamming the door so that the old walls shook.

Downstairs in the kitchen quarters the servants were sitting whispering to one another.

"Listen, could you hear that? It's that young lady again! If you ask me she's nothing but a changeling! God bless Lady Sidsela, our poor, dear mistress!" they said, making the sign of the cross.

Upstairs, Lady Sidsela sighed heavily. Her husband had died many years ago, when her daughter was a baby, and shortly afterwards she herself had fallen so ill that all hope of recovery was abandoned. After many months of illness she had survived, but by the time she was strong enough to see her little daughter again, she did not recognise her. The gentle, happy baby had become a sour, evil-tempered girl, so that her mother often wondered if she could be the same child.

"Perhaps the loss of her father and the fear of losing her mother as well caused this drastic change," the kindhearted Lady Sidsela told herself. And she was determined never to show the slightest doubt, or to be impatient towards her daughter.

Lady Sidsela looked out through the window across the gardens, fields and hills of her wide estate. She fixed her attention on a huge boulder lying ominously in the middle of an empty field: the mysterious Magle-Stone.

It was said that under this stone some trolls had made their dwellings, and it was considered a fearful, dangerous place, shunned by all. In spite of her good intentions she could not help the suspicion growing in her mind that there might be some connection between her daughter's strange behaviour and this uncanny place.

Once a year on Christmas Eve, when everyone was safe at home, the trolls were believed to hold a great feast. Lady Sidsela made up her mind to try and find out what went on there.

The next Christmas Eve, Lady Sidsela promised the best horse in the stable and a fine garment to any of her servants who would dare to visit the Magle-Stone that very night. A young, bold servant bravely offered to go and find out what happened there, and went down to the stable, saddled a horse and set out to the Stone. It was a dark night, with not even the tiniest little star to help him find his way. As he was riding along he saw a faint light glowing from the mysterious Stone. When he came closer a cloud of smoke billowed from beneath it, and suddenly with a dull crash the huge boulder swung slowly up into the air supported by four massive golden pillars.

Underneath, the servant saw a vast hall filled with a swarm of ugly misshapen trolls, jumping and swinging their tails about in wild dances. Some of them caught sight of their uninvited visitor and pointed at him. Immediately the dance stopped and the trolls crowded round the intruder. A young troll-girl came up to him bearing a costly cushion on which lay a drinking-horn and a pipe and asked him to drink a toast to the health of the Troll-King, and then blow three times with the pipe.

The young man was just about to do what he was asked, when he became aware of a young girl at his side making secret warning signs at him. Without a moment's hesitation he turned his horse and set off at full gallop towards the castle, pursued by hundreds of trolls. Not until he was safe on the other side of the moat and the drawbridge was pulled up did the trolls cease their chase.

That night Lady Sidsela could not sleep a wink. When she heard the thunder of a galloping horse approaching, she rose from her bed, flung a gown over her shoulders and went downstairs, eager to hear the reports from her servant. Trembling and panting, the young man told her about the strange things he had seen under the Magle-Stone, and about his narrow escape from the trolls.

Lady Sidsela brooded for a long time on what she had heard from her brave servant about his visit to the trolls. She longed to get some more information of the trolls' doings under the boulder-stone, but the young man did not dare to try a second visit to the trolls, and no one else offered to set out on such a dangerous adventure.

Time passed by, and once again Christmas drew near. The bad temper of the young lady of Ljungby Castle had not softened, and the old walls often resounded with her outbursts of shrewishness. Trembling servants hid behind corners when they saw her approaching, trying to avoid her fits of fury and scornful remarks.

Lady Sidsela decided that her young daughter now had reached a suitable age to think about getting married.

"Marriage to a kind and noble knight may work wonders for any young girl," she thought to herself. So she sent her servants to all the castles in the surrounding countryside with an invitation to the young knights and noblemen to spend Christmas at Ljungby.

At Christmas-time the castle was in a frenzy of activity, for so many young men had accepted Lady Sidsela's invitation. Amongst them was a gallant young knight, Sir Sten Boson. He had heard many stories about the annual celebrations of the trolls under the Magle-Stone near Ljungby Castle, and when he was told what had happened the year before he decided to discover for himself what was going on under that mysterious boulder.

Just before midnight on Christmas Eve he revealed his intention to his hostess and the other guests at the castle, then he went down to the stable and saddled his horse.

It was pitch dark, and the sky was starless just as it had been a year ago, but now a keen wind swept whistling and howling over the fields and the night seemed black and ominous. Shuddering, Sir Sten drew his cloak tighter round his shoulders and set out across the bare fields, for that year there had not yet been any snow.

Soon, however, the young knight could see a faint flickering light and turning his horse towards it, he galloped on. As he drew nearer he saw a round spot of light on the ground. Above the light a cloud of smoke hung over the huge stone whose outlines were vaguely visible in the darkness.

The knight heard a sudden crack and the earth seemed to revolve under his feet: the huge stone rose of its own accord resting on the enormous golden pillars and hung like a gigantic canopy over a scene more strange and uncanny than any human ever witnessed.

The darkness was pierced by the flames of a hundred blazing fires around which the knight saw swarms of trolls jumping up and down, swinging their arms and legs in some mysterious dance while they yelled and shouted in a strange rhythmical way. One of them caught sight of the intruder and stopped dancing to point at him, and the next moment they had surrounded him like a cloud of angry bees. They crowded round him, jostling and poking him, mocking him and pulling threatening faces. Suddenly, they moved back to make way for a young troll-girl who came up and offered him a drinking horn richly engraved and decorated with silver and a fine little ivory pipe made in the shape of a dragon.

The troll-girl said, "Take this horn and drink a toast to the Troll-King, then blow the pipe three times."

Sir Sten took both horn and pipe out of her hands and was just going to do as he was told, when he was aware of the fair figure of a young girl close at his side. Warningly she whispered in his ear, "Young knight, take care, don't taste a drop!" And then, hardly audible, she added, "Please take me away from here!"

Sir Sten emptied the horn behind his back, and quick as lightning he put the horn and the pipe inside his jacket, seized the girl, and lifting her up on his horse in front of him, set off at full gallop across the field.

When the trolls realised that they had not only been robbed of their fair prisoner, but also of their most precious treasure, they set up such a furious scream that it made the blood go cold in the veins of the fleeing knight and the young girl.

Soon the trolls were fast on the heels of the riders who feared that at any moment they would be pulled down from the horse and killed.

"Don't follow the furrows, ride across! Ride across!" the girl whispered in the knight's ear. Sir Sten turned his horse so that the tracks of its hoofs crossed the ridges of the earth.

Instantly the trolls stood rooted to the spot. They shouted and yelled, they twisted and turned, and they raised their fists

threateningly after the robber, but they were not able to move from the spot. There on the ground in front of them the tracks formed a long row of crosses, and the sign of the cross prevented them from further pursuit and made them powerless.

Sir Sten soon left the shouting trolls far behind, and all danger seemed to be over. Just as they reached the drawbridge his horse shuddered and then collapsed and died. Terribly upset he examined his dear horse to find out what had happened. He discovered a few bare spots on its skin, and remorsefully remembered how some drops had splashed on to the beast while he was emptying the dangerous contents of the troll-horn.

He mourned his faithful horse which had bravely carried

himself and the young girl away from their terrible pursuers. Then he turned to the girl at his side and gratefully thanked her for saving him from sharing the fate of the horse. Taking the young girl by the hand he led her across the drawbridge into the castle.

Lady Sidsela was still up waiting for her guest to return from his daring adventure. When the young knight came walking into the hall with the beautiful young girl by his side, Lady Sidsela gazed spell-bound at them. She felt her heart beating heavily when she looked at the girl, her eyes filled with tears and sobbing she called out, "Bridget! Bridget! My own rightful daughter! My true darling daughter!" And flinging her arms round the young girl's neck, she kissed her tenderly over and over again, the tears running down her cheeks.

Suddenly, Lady Sidsela started up and cried out, "But the other one! Who then is the other one?"

All three of them turned round and caught sight of the former young Lady of Ljungby Castle. There she stood behind them with a scornful sneer on her broad mouth. Putting two fingers into her mouth she gave a sharp whistle. Then the stunned and terrified onlookers saw her fly right up in the air and disappear out of the open window.

With a deep sigh of relief Lady Sidsela said, "Thank goodness for that," and making the sign of the cross she added, "Well, at least we know the reason for all our troubles." Lady Sidsela went to bed more pleased and happy than she had been for many, many years.

She had not been in bed for very long before she woke up to the most dreadful noise she had ever heard. Going to the window, she drew back the curtains and looked out. It had been snowing for quite a while, for everything was wrapped in white like a soft white fleece. But that only made the sight that caught her eyes so much worse. Cold shivers ran up her spine, for there, on the other side of the moat, she saw hundreds of trolls like black shadows against the white snow, jumping up and down screaming, "Give us back our horn and pipe! Give us back our horn and pipe, or disaster will befall you and your whole family!"

Lady Sidsela hurriedly shut the window, closed the curtains again, and went to bed. But all night through she heard the terrible noise of the trolls.

The following night the trolls came again outside her window, and this time there seemed twice as many as before. Their noise was so terrific that she could not stand it any longer, but went up to the window and opened the curtains.

Everything was still white outside, so Lady Sidsela could clearly distinguish that among the trolls on the other side of the moat was the Troll-King himself holding out to her another horn filled with gold and silver as he shouted, "Give me back my horn and pipe! Look, I offer you this horn instead, together with all the treasures it contains! Please, give me back my horn and pipe!"

But Lady Sidsela was determined not to give them their evil powers again and unshaken she shut the window, drew the curtains and went to bed. There was no sleep for her that night either for the trolls went on shouting as long as it was dark.

On the third night the trolls were there again, in even greater numbers than before, crowding their black, ugly shapes over all the surrounding fields and hills. Their noise was deafening and more terrifying than before. Lady Sidsela could not help it, against her will she went up to the window, opened it and looked out.

Again the Troll-King was standing on the other side of the moat, surrounded by all his horrible subjects. He lifted his hands beseechingly towards Lady Sidsela, yelling out, "Give me back my horn and pipe! Or promise me at least never to let them be taken away from this estate. Let me take a vow from you that they will stay here for ever!"

Lady Sidsela made the vow, resolutely shut the window, drew the curtains, and went to bed. Now the noise ceased and everything was quiet.

Some months later there was a wedding at Ljungby Castle. The young knight Sten Boson was married to Lady Bridget Ulfstand. Not long afterwards Lady Sidsela died, then after a few years the whole Ulfstand family died out, and new owners came to the castle.

There are many stories about how later owners have tried to take away the horn and pipe from the estate, and how they have then been haunted by the trolls until the treasures were returned to the castle. And many are the changes which have taken place since the Ulfstand family died, but still the horn and pipe, which are said to have been stolen from the trolls, are kept on the estate and shown to visitors as its most precious treasure. And still the mysterious Magle-Stone stands in the field of Trolle Ljungby, which is the name of the old estate today.

# The Golden Goose
## A story from Flanders

ONCE UPON A TIME there was a little boy whose name was Jean.
There is nothing remarkable about that, for there isn't a boy's
name more popular in the whole of Flanders. But this little Jean
was an orphan who had been found one morning under a
walnut tree, where his parents, for some reason or other, had
left him. And because he was found under a walnut tree he was
called Walnut-Jean to distinguish him from other boys with
that name.

As soon as little Walnut-Jean was old enough to be of some
use he was set to work. His job was to look after sheep, so he
became a shepherd and got his own little corner in the hay
loft where he could sleep. Though he seldom had anything else
to eat apart from potatoes and some dry bread, he grew up
into a strong and healthy boy. He was friendly and kindhearted but unfortunately he had very few brains. Some unkind
people found him so stupid they started calling him "The Calf"
for they thought him as innocent and simple as a new-born calf.

Not many miles from where Jean lived was the village of Hergnies. It was famous throughout Flanders for its big, fat geese, and flocks of these fattened geese could be seen everywhere in the neighbourhood. When Jean drove his sheep home every evening, he passed many rich farmhouses, from where the delicious smell of roast goose was wafted out to him. He sniffed the tasty smell hungrily, envying the lucky people who could afford to eat roast goose.

He made up his mind that the only thing he wanted in the world was to eat roast goose too.

"When I'm grown-up I shall go to Hergnies and eat roast goose," he told himself every day.

One autumn evening when he had driven his sheep home, he didn't go back to his hayloft as usual but set out for Hergnies. His longing for goose had been too much for him, and he felt he just had to go and eat some.

He wandered along asking his way whenever he happened to see someone. Late in the evening he came to a farmhouse. As there was no-one about on the road he went up to the house and knocked on the door. The farmer's wife opened it and behind her Jean could see people sitting round a table having their supper.

"Please, could you show me the way to Hergnies, dear Mother?"

"Yes, certainly, but isn't it rather late at this time of the day? You are not in such a hurry that you want to set off right now, are you?"

"Well, yes I am. For more than ten years I've wanted to go to Hergnies to eat roast goose, so you will understand that I've been waiting long enough. I've put off my journey so many times I am determined to go this time."

The farmer's wife was surprised at such an answer. She

looked at the tall, healthy-looking boy from head to foot. He certainly looked a bit simple but good-natured and honest as well.

"What is your name?" she asked him.

"Most people called me Calf, but . . ."

"Yes, yes, I understand perfectly," she interrupted him laughingly. "Listen, my boy, you seem to be a decent young chap, and besides, you are tall and strong. Our servant has just left, would you like to take his place?"

"Would you let me eat goose then?" asked Jean.

"As a matter of fact we are going to have goose for dinner, this coming Sunday. I was going to send a message to my cousin who lives at Hergnies, for a fine fat goose, but now you could go tomorrow and collect it. We will eat it on the feast of Saint Calixtus, and then we all shall go to his chapel to see the Procession of the Cured. Does this arrangement suit you?"

"Oh, yes, certainly it does," was the enthusiastic answer.

"Well then, come in and join us for supper, will you?" asked the kind woman.

To the tired and half-starved boy this invitation seemed like a dream. He certainly did not need to be asked twice, but sat right down and ate a hearty meal. Afterwards he was shown to the barn where he was to spend the night.

The following morning as dawn was breaking the farmer's wife went to the barn where Jean still lay sleeping in the hay.

"Come on, get up! you have a long way ahead of you," she shouted out to him. Before he left he got something to drink and a piece of bread for his breakfast. He put another piece of bread in his pocket, to eat later in the day when he was hungry. The farmer's wife carefully described the way he had to take to find her cousin, and finally she said, "You must bring home from my cousin, not just the fat goose, but also seven-and-a-half-gallons of rye-seed. Don't forget that will you?"

"No, I'll try to remember it," promised Jean, and started on his way to Hergnies.

When he left the farmhouse the cock stood on the thatched roof crowing loudly, calling out to everybody that now the new day had begun. And this new day was a Friday.

"The day after tomorrow I'm going to eat goose," Jean thought to himself. And while he was thinking this, he kept repeating loudly "Seven-and-a-half-gallons, seven-and-a-half-gallons . . .", so he wouldn't forget his errand to the farmer's cousin.

While he was walking along saying this to himself, he passed a field where a farmer was busy sowing his seed. The farmer was just calculating how much his soil would produce next year when he hear a voice calling out, "Seven-and-a-half-gallons."

"Thank you my lad," he retorted scornfully, "you should rather say 'May there be a hundred'."

His words muddled the whole thing up in the head of poor Jean, who always had difficulty in remembering more than one thing at a time. So now instead of saying "Seven-and-a-half-gallons," he started muttering "May there be a hundred, may there be a hundred."

Some way off he met "Big Thomas", a shepherd whom he knew was a fierce and conceited fellow. Today he was worse than ever, for a wolf, which had been a plague to all the shepherds in the neighbourhood, had been caught by Big Thomas's dog and then finally killed by Thomas himself.

"May there be a hundred, may there be a hundred," Walnut-Jean went on repeating as he passed.

"May there be a hundred wolves! Shame on you, you lousy Calf, you should say, 'It served him right'!" shouted Big Thomas fiercely.

"It served him right! It served him right!" bellowed Jean and ran off, afraid that Big Thomas would set on him.

While he went along saying "It served him right, it served him right," he saw a church-tower not far away.

"Right," he thought, "here is the first village I have to pass." He hurried on and was walking through its narrow street. Out of the church came a bridal couple surrounded by the wedding-guests. The bride was known to everybody as a rich and haughty girl, and it was also said that the bridegroom, an ill-tempered man, only wanted her money.

"It served him right, it served him right," Walnut-Jean kept saying loudly as he passed.

"Whom does it serve right? Me?" roared the bridegroom angrily, shaking his fist at Jean.

Then one of the guests took pity on Jean, and whispered in his ear, "You fool, you should say, 'Everybody should go ahead and do the same!'"

"Everybody should go ahead and do the same. Everybody should go ahead and do the same," repeated Jean whose thoughts were more confused than ever.

Soon he left the village behind and was walking along the country road again. Suddenly, he saw a lot of people running in the same direction. Like most boys he was curious to see what was going on, so he joined the hurrying crowd. He discovered that the attraction was a house on fire. People swarmed up to help put it out. They discovered the man who had deliberately started the fire and as Jean came up two strong fellows came dragging him along.

"Everybody should go ahead and do the same," Jean kept saying loudly.

"What on earth are you saying? Surely you don't want to encourage people to set houses on fire, do you? You can get hanged for less!" a threatening voice shouted at him.

"You should say instead, 'May God let the fire go out'," a friendlier voice from the crowd advised him. And poor Jean had no choice but to repeat, "May God let the fire go out! May God let the fire go out!" And he ran away as if the fire were on his own heels.

He did not slacken his pace until he came to the next village. Now he thought he had at last come to Hergnies. He walked along the road happily repeating "May God let the fire go out," until he came to a blacksmith's shop. All morning the blacksmith had been busy trying to make a fire on his forge, and was in a terrible mood. Finally he managed to light a feeble, little blue flame.

"May God let the fire go out!" he heard a loud voice saying outside his shop. This made him livid. He lost control of himself, took his hammer and flung it at the head of poor Jean, who fell unconscious on the ground.

The blow would have killed anyone else, but Jean's thick head stood the strain. Some kind people rushed to his help, and carried him to a farmhouse, where he soon recovered. The only damage he got from the blow was a bump on his forehead. The kind farmer asked him where he was going and what his errand was.

"I've come here to Hergnies to eat roasted goose," he answered.

"Poor lad, do you think this is Hergnies? There's another twelve miles walk from here," he answered. "I'm well acquainted with the place, and many times I've joined the Procession of the Cured to Saint Calixtus chapel at Hergnies."

To comfort Jean for his misfortunes the good farmer gave him a whole sheaf of corn, as well as something to eat and drink before he set out again on his way to Hergnies. When Jean was ready to leave the farmhouse, the kind farmer carefully pointed out the direction he had to take.

However, it was not long before Jean was totally at a loss again as to how to find his way. It must have been about noon, and Jean felt hungry and tired. He sat down on the ground with his sheaf of corn beside him. Leaning his head against a tree he sat munching a piece of his bread, and before long he had fallen asleep.

After a while he woke to find to his horror that a rooster and some hens were picking out the grains of his sheaf. He burst into loud wails and moans, until the owner of the rooster and the hens who happened to be passing came running to see what was wrong. Feeling sorry for the poor lad, he said, "You may keep the rooster as compensation for your sheaf of corn."

"A thousand thanks to you!" said Jean very pleased. He took the rooster, tied his feet together, flung him over his shoulder and continued his walk.

It was a hot day and the sun beat down on Jean as he was walking along with his burden on his back. In the afternoon he felt tired and hungry again so he put his rooster down in a field and sat beside him on a fence by the roadside. He ate another bit of bread as he rested but didn't notice that a cow was grazing close by. The cow found the rooster was in her way, so she gave him a kick as he lay bound up on the grass, and then trod on him so that the poor, ill-treated rooster expired.

When Jean saw what had happened he groaned and cried bitterly. "Oh dear! Why do I always have such bad luck! First I was almost killed, then I got a sheaf of corn, and a rooster ate all the grains, then I got the rooster, and now a cow has killed the rooster.

"Do for heaven's sake stop that crying, and take the cow

then!" said an irritated voice. It was the squire himself who had heard Jean's crying and had had enough of it.

"A thousand thanks to you, sir," said Jean who felt quite happy again. He bowed low to the squire, took the cow and went away. Soon Walnut-Jean was proudly walking along the road, feeling quite an important person now that he had become an owner of a cow.

At last he saw a farmhouse by the side of the road and went up to it. He knocked on the door and asked for a place where he and his cow could spend the night. He was shown to the stable where he soon dropped off to sleep.

Early next morning he woke up to the sound of a terrible din. A strong and pretty-looking maid was milking his cow. The cow had been stung by a wasp and swung its tail with all its force to get rid of the fierce little thing. Instead, its tail hit the girl right between her eyes making her see a thousand stars. The girl was bad-tempered at the best of times, but now she was simply furious. "Just you wait! I'll . . . I'll . . ." screamed the maid. Hardly able to draw breath, she took a pitch-fork and beat the cow for all she was worth, over and over again until it fell to the ground, stone dead.

At this sight Jean began his lamentations again. He went to the farmer complaining of the disgraceful behaviour of his maid.

"I'm indeed a most unhappy creature, always haunted by bad luck! First they nearly killed me, then I got a sheaf of corn and a rooster ate all the grains, then I got the rooster, and a cow killed the rooster, then I got the cow, and now your maid has killed the cow," he said sobbing.

"Stop that crying and take the maid then!" said the farmer who was glad to get rid of the bad-tempered girl.

Now Jean was quite satisfied again. With the aid of the

farmer he managed to tie the maid's feet together and put her into the sack. As he walked along with the heavy sack on his back Jean talked to the maid to try and calm her down for she kicked and yelled constantly.

"Be quiet, my dear," he said soothingly, "when we get to Hergnies I shall marry you and we shall eat roast goose together."

This time he was at last on the right way to Hergnies, but now he was too tired to walk any further with his heavy and troublesome burden. He stopped at the first inn he set eyes on, and leaving his sack outside went in to rest a while, and have something to eat and drink.

At a table inside three gay fellows were sitting watching Jean come in. Suddenly one of them cried, "I say look at that! Am I tipsy or is that sack out there really moving?"

"My word, and it's making the most extraordinary funny movements for an ordinary sack," said another.

"Why not let's go and see what's up?" said the third. So all three rose from the table to go and examine the sack, followed by a big dog which belonged to one of them.

Soon the three friends stood round the sack which was moving about in the court-yard. One of them seized it while another untied the string round the neck of the sack. To their great surprise they saw a pretty maid crawling out. They helped to untie the string round her feet, urging her to tell them how she came to be inside the sack. She told them her story and said she hadn't the slightest desire to marry a tramp like Jean.

"Run off then, as fast as you can," they advised her, and off she went as fast as her legs would carry her.

"What are we going to put in the sack instead of the girl?" asked one.

"Let's put the dog in," suggested another.

"But I don't want to lose him," protested the owner.

"Why should you? As soon as he gets a chance he'll come running back to you. Besides, why don't we follow the lad for a bit and see what happens?" suggested the first.

So they put the dog into the sack, and as long as he could smell his master he kept quiet.

When Walnut-Jean had finished his meal he came out again, took his sack on his back and continued his walk without even noticing that his burden was now lighter. Finally he arrived at Hergnies. The first thing he wanted to do was to go straight to the parish priest to get married. But then he remembered that he had quite forgotten to ask the girl whether she agreed to marry him.

He put down the sack, and while he was untying it, asked, "Listen, my dear girl, do you want to marry me?" A loud bark answered him. Jean got such a surprise that he let go of the string. Out jumped the big dog, his jaws wide open, ready to fly at Jean's throat. Frightened, Jean fled and only escaped by climbing up a willow tree, but the heavy weight of Jean broke the branch in two and it fell with a terrible crack.

Scared by the sound, the dog turned and putting his tail between his legs he set off to his master as if he was being chased by a bear. Jean, who was flung to the ground together with the tree, thought that this was the very end of him. He was surprised to discover that both head and limbs still were in their right places. He tried to get up—and rose easily to his feet. When he discovered that he could even move and walk as before, he was convinced that he must be still alive. He turned round and looked at the cracked tree. Suddenly, he noticed that there was something sparkling and glittering in the hollow stump. He pushed his hand into the hollow and pulled it out. He had caught a little goose with feathers of pure gold.

"Well, here is the goose I've come to fetch!" he cried in delight. "At last I'm going to eat roast goose!"

With the golden goose under his arm he went straight to the nearest inn to have it roasted, quite forgetting the poor farmer's wife who had sent him to fetch her fat goose and the seven-and-a-half-gallons of rye-seed; and she is probably still watching for them this very day.

As Jean arrived at the inn he found it very crowded. People usually made a halt here, so they could continue their pilgrimage to Saint Calixtus' Chapel the following morning.

When Jean went to the landlord and asked to have his goose roasted, the landlord answered with a snort of fury: "D'ye mean me to roast a goose of gold? Are you pulling my leg, or are you mad?"

"Well, if I can't eat my goose," thought Jean disappointed, "then I can at least give it to Saint Calixtus. Perhaps he will give me a real one, that I can eat instead."

He had a meal at the inn, and then went as usual to the stable to sleep. Before lying down in the hay he thought he had better be careful with this new treasure, so he took a piece of string and tied one end round the goose, and the other one round his wrist, to be sure he was not robbed of the precious bird while he slept.

The landlord had three young daughters who helped him serve the guests. Every night when they had finished their day's work, they went up to their room to sleep. But tonight they could not get a wink of sleep for they lay awake thinking of the young lad with the wonderful golden goose. All three of them had just one wish: to get a glimpse of the strange, beautiful bird at close quarters.

Early in the morning at the cock's first crow the eldest of the girls rose from her bed and said, "It's too hot in here, I can't stay in bed any longer." And she stole out of the bedroom and went down to the stable. The moon was still up in the sky, and she saw the golden bird glittering like a star in the bright moonlight. After admiring it for quite a while, she was overcome with a powerful longing to pull out just one of its golden feathers. She stretched out her hand to do so—but a terrible thing happened, for as soon as she touched the goose she just could not move her hand away. It simply stuck to the goose and the goose was tied to the boy's wrist. So the girl had to stay where she was.

When the cock crowed the second time the second sister woke up. Seeing that her eldest sister had left the room, she, too, rose from her bed.

"I can't stand the heat in here any longer, I must get up!" she said and left the room. She thought she knew where she could find her sister, and went straight down to the stable.

"What are you doing in here?" she asked, pulling her sister by her sleeve, but then she, too, was stuck and just could not move from the spot.

The cock crowed the third time, and the landlord's youngest daughter woke up. "Now the cock is wishing good morning to Saint Calixtus, and it's time for me to get up," she said to herself.

And a fine Sunday morning it was. The sun had risen like a golden ball above the horizon when the girl went down to the stable. Here she found her two elder sisters beside the golden goose which glittered in the shining rays of the sun.

"Take care! Take care!" the two sisters called out to her. "They want me to be careful not to wake the boy," she thought when she saw Jean still sleeping in the hay, his back turned towards them. So she crept quietly up to her sisters. Touching the hand of one of them she bent forward to get a closer look at the wonderful bird. Alas! She found that she, too, was unable to remove her hand. She just had to stand there beside her sisters.

After a while Jean woke up. Yawning widely he turned to stretch himself, but an uncomfortable string prevented him from doing so. He untied the string, stretched himself and brushed the hay off his ragged trousers and dirty shirt. Then he turned his head and suddenly noticed the three girls round his golden goose. Immediately he remembered everything that had happened the day before, and it flashed across his mind that the three girls were trying to steal his bird. He hurriedly picked up his treasure and holding it tightly under his arm he took to his heels out through the stable-door and down into the road, unaware of the three girls who came running after him.

"Stop, oh please do stop!" they panted breathlessly.

This only strengthened Jean's suspicions. They wanted, of course, his goose, but he was determined not to let them have it, so he increased his speed instead. But Jean could not keep this pace up indefinitely. He was finally forced to give in to the panting and crying girls, and agreed to slow down on condition that they showed him the way to the chapel of Saint Calixtus.

A little further down the road they passed the parish priest, the curate, two chaplains, the deacon, the organist, the organ-blower, the bell-ringer and the choir-boys. They were all on their way to Saint Calixtus' Chapel.

When the parish priest saw the girls running behind the young lad he called out, "Aren't you ashamed of yourselves, girls, to run after a boy like that!" And catching the youngest of the sisters by her skirt he hoped to stop her from this shameful behaviour. But, alas! He now found that he, too, was stuck and was obliged to follow Jean.

"Father, Father, what has happened to you? Where are you going?" cried the curate, running after the prist to call him back to his duties, and he seized him by his long gown. Now he, too, was unable to get free!

Seeing the curate struggling to tear the priest away from the girls, the two chaplains, the deacon, the organist, the organ-blower, the bell-ringer and the choir boys joined hands, trying with united efforts to get the parish priest free—but instead they were now all stuck to each other, helplessly struggling and kicking to get free.

Completely unaware of what was going on behind his back Jean tightened his grip round the goose. There was only one thought in his mind; to leave his golden goose at the feet of Saint Calixtus. The rest of the company had no choice, they just had to keep up with him as best they could.

Of all the saints in Flanders there was no one in those days more famous than Saint Calixtus. On his feast day, crowds of people made pilgrimages to his chapel near Hergnies, for it was said that he could cure the sick and the lame. No wonder, then, that many came to be cured. But there were many more who had already been cured and who wanted to show their grati-tude to the Saint for answering their prayers by taking part in the Procession of the Cured. It was indeed a strange sight. There came a long line of crooked, hunch-backed, crippled and squinting people. But they were in fact just acting the ailments they had suffered, to make their thanksgiving for being cured. They hobbled along to the chapel of Saint Calixtus where they flung away their sticks and crutches, bandages and plasters. They straightened their backs and limbs and walked away as strong and upright as other people, to show the miracle of being cured. It was this spectacle that had become so popular, and crowds poured in to the town to watch.

This year more people had arrived than ever before, because there was a rumour that the King and Queen of the Netherlands were to come with their daughter to watch the procession. This poor Princess, it was said, could not laugh. She had been given everything a child could wish for, right from the day she was born. Toys, sweets and all kinds of amusements had been lavished upon her, so that now she was grown-up she was bored to death with everything. The most famous jokers and clowns were called to the court, and had performed all their tricks and jokes in vain. But she was fed up with them all, and nothing would make her laugh.

At last the King proclaimed that any man who was able to make the Princess laugh should marry her. Some had tried, but there were not many who wanted to marry a girl, Princess though she was, who was so dull and spoilt that nothing could make her laugh. As a last chance the King and Queen decided to let the Princess watch the Procession of the Cured, for it was well-known that the antics and capers of the cured cripples amused anyone who saw it.

The King and Queen, with the Princess, had been watching the procession the whole morning. They had seen the strangest figures passing by, funnier than any clown or joker they had ever seen. The courtiers and the ladies-of-honour had been roaring with laughter, so had the King and Queen, but the Princess had merely yawned and been as bored as usual.

The King at last gave up all hope of ever seeing his daughter laugh, and decided there was no point staying in the chapel any longer, so he gave the order to arrange for their journey home. Just as they were bringing the horses, everyone stopped talking, and turned their heads in the same direction. They saw a strange procession approaching: a boy came running in front, holding a golden goose under his arm; after him struggled three young girls, a fat priest, a tall thin curate, two chaplains, a deacon, an organist, an organ-blower, a bell-ringer and a long row of choir-boys. They seemed stuck together, though they were wriggling and kicking to get free, and stumbling and treading on each other's toes and heels as they were forced to keep pace with the boy.

There was not one of the royal party who did not laugh at them; even the Princess twitched her mouth in what was almost a smile. This sight was indeed something out of the ordinary, and the Princess seemed to enjoy it so much that she followed the company—at some distance—into the chapel. Here, Jean put the goose down at the feet of Saint Calixtus. Immediately, the magic of the goose was broken. It happened so quickly that as the struggling procession was suddenly set free, they all tumbled back on the ground, flat on their backs, with their legs waving in the air.

The three young girls, the fat priest, the tall thin curate and the others all screamed with laughter at the ridiculous sight they made.

And indeed they were a laughing stock. The Princess fell roaring with laughter into the arms of the Queen. And the King flung his arm round Jean's neck and called out in delight: "You shall marry her! You shall marry her!" Jean, not understanding what was happening, asked stupidly "Who? Whom am I to marry?"

"The Princess of course! My daughter!" cried the King.

Jean turned and caught sight of the pretty Princess who was standing with her arms round her mother's neck, helpless with laughter, and found no objection to make. He found her even better than the farmer's maid. So they decided to hold the wedding in a week's time.

Herds of geese were sent to the wedding from Hergnies, and now Jean could eat roast goose to his heart's content. During the wedding feast the King proclaimed Jean a Prince and heir to the throne.

As King and ruler Jean was quite a success, and many a wiser man has done worse; for he just let people do as they wanted and repeated what his Chancellors told him, so everyone was pleased with him. And when things did not turn out well no-one had cause to blame the King. Jean lived happily with his Queen and his people ever after.

# The Dream
## A story from Transylvania

EARLY ONE MORNING a poor peasant and his three sons were
sitting at their breakfast table, having a humble meal before
starting their daily work. The eldest son yawned and said:

"You'll never guess what a peculiar dream I had last night!"

"How funny," said the second son, "I too have had a most
extraordinary dream."

"I'll bet that none of you have had even half as strange a
dream as I had last night," retorted the youngest.

"Well then, my sons, let me hear about your dreams!"
urged the father.

So the eldest son began: "I dreamt I was invited to a party
and there I had a wonderful time. The table was laden with all
kinds of delicious food. First we had six different kinds of fish,
and then we had roast chicken, with thick juicy chunks of roast
ham and beef, and when everything was finished the table was
filled again with all kinds of new and marvellous dishes, the
names of which I don't even know. When I had tasted every-

thing and left the table, I was so stout when I banged my chest, it was like beating a drum, and the sparrows were so frightened that they fell down from the trees."

"Well, my son, if you have eaten so much last night, you need no other food today," was the father's answer.

"And your dream?" he asked turning to his second son.

"Dear father, I dreamt I went to the shoemaker's to buy a pair of boots. And I bought a pair of the finest shiny leather with elegant silver spurs. I put them on and clicked my heels together and the sound rang out so loud, I thought it must have been heard seven kingdoms off."

"Well, my son, you might have had a pair of boots like that last night, but this morning you must content yourself with the pair you've got, for I can't afford to buy you any others this year," answered his father. "And what was your dream, my son?" he asked turning to his youngest boy.

"That I won't tell you," was the impertinent answer. The father gave his son a straight look. "I've warned you before about talking to me like this, it's a bad habit of yours and it's time you learned to be obedient to your father." But the boy remained silent. "If you won't tell me your dream at once I'll beat you black and blue for your obstinacy!" roared the father, and went to fetch a stick to carry out his threat.

To flee is shameful, but it helps, runs the old saying. So the boy set off as fast as his legs would carry him, out through the door and down the road. His father came chasing close on his heels, his stick in hand. He followed him down the narrow country road, but the boy was just turning into the highway when his father managed to seize him, and they almost fell under a splendid coach which was driving past. In the coach sat the King himself and his daughter, the pretty little Princess. The royal coach was forced to jerk suddenly to a halt, so as not to run over the two combatants.

The King looked out angrily to see what had made his horses stop so suddenly. When he saw the elder man beating the boy, he called out, "Hullo! you there! What is going on?"

The father was so busy flogging his son, that he hardly noticed the coach and still less who was inside. Not until he heard the words did he look up and realising who it was, he made a bow so deep that his head almost seemed to touch the ground.

"Your Majesty," he said panting, "my son has been very rude. I'm just giving him a sound thrashing. He refuses to tell me his dream."

"We'll see about that," said the King. "If I give you this purse of sovereigns, let the boy come with me. I'll certainly make him speak."

The father who never saw so much money in his life, was glad to have the purse, and returned home very pleased.

Meanwhile the Princess sat in her coach, her eyes glittering with delight at this unusual delay to their ride. She was bored to death with the dull early morning drives with her father. Admiringly, she watched the slender, handsome youth with his jet-black hair and daring brown eyes.

The King urged the boy to tell him his dream. But when he only shook his head refusing to say anything, the Princess chuckled to herself, amused at the thought that someone dared to resist her father, the King.

The King ordered the boy to come with them to the castle, where he thought he would soon make the boy speak.

When the Princess heard this, it gave her heart a jump, for she thought the handsome youth would now sit up in the coach beside her. But her face dropped when the two footmen at the back of the coach took the boy between them.

They continued their drive to the royal castle. The boy was now treated as a prisoner, and after being made to wait a few hours he was brought into a large hall where the King sat surrounded by his knights and courtiers.

"Now young man, I hope for your sake that you are going to tell me about your strange dream last night," said the King encouragingly. But the boy still said nothing.

"Do you know what it means to refuse to obey your King?" the King continued more sternly.

There was still no answer from the boy. One of the courtiers stepped forward, and said severely, "We call it treason, and to commit a crime like this is forbidden on pain of death."

The King felt relieved, thinking that this would make the obstinate boy more agreeable. However, it seemed to make no difference to the youth, for he still said nothing.

Then the King lost patience, and ordered the guards to throw the boy into a tower which was to be completely walled up by the stonemason. "Now," the King said turning to the youth, "You'll have plenty of time to regret your disobedience to your King."

The prisoner received the news of his severe punishment quite calmly. The King's pretty daughter, however, no longer smiled at the boy's courage. Her rosy cheeks grew paler and paler. She knew that this meant a tower where there was neither door nor window. There the prisoner was to be walled in and starved to death.

When the youth was taken away by the guards, the Princess thought of a plan to save him. She stole down to the tower, and secretly put a golden coin in the hand of the mason whose job it was to take out some stones in the tower to let the prisoner climb in, and replace them again as soon as he was inside. She told him to keep a couple of stones loose, so it would be possible for her to take them out and put food into the tower for the prisoner.

Every evening the Princess now went to the tower bringing the youth a basket filled with delicious food from the King's own table, so that he always had something to eat.

Time passed and one day seven snow-white horses, all exactly alike, were sent to the King. They came from the mighty Tartar Prince with the demand that unless someone could guess the ages of each, he would destroy the whole country and kill all the inhabitants, except the Princess, whom he intended to marry.

The King was terrified, and gathered all the wise men in his country, to hold council with them. But they could not help him. The whole court was seized with fear and despair.

The King's daughter was so upset that when she brought food to the youth that evening, the tears streamed down her cheeks.

"What is it that makes you so sad, my fair Princess?" asked the youth. The Princess told him the whole story about the horses, and the threat which accompanied them.

"Dry your tears and don't worry any longer! Tell your father to put oats in seven cribs, and in each crib the oats must be of a different year's crops. In the first crib there must be the crops from last year's harvest, and in the second one oats from the year before and so on. The horses will then choose oats of the year of their birth, if they are free to choose their own places. They will then be lined up in order of age; but you must not tell your father who has given you this advice. Tell him you got it in a dream."

The Princess did as she was told, the King followed the advice, and the horses were sent back with a statement of their age. The Tartar Prince could not deny that the answer was correct, however much he would have liked to do so.

But some time later he sent a rod to the King with the same terrible threat unless someone could find out which end of the rod was cut nearest the root of the tree.

Again the King and his people were afraid and so was his pretty daughter. That night she went to the youth in the tower and told him all her troubles.

"Sweetest Princess, don't be so sad! Tell your father to find out the middle of the rod carefully. He must tie a piece of string round it, and hang the string from the ceiling, and whichever end was cut nearest the root will sink down towards the ground, for it is the heaviest part."

The Princess went to her father and told him that in a new dream she had learnt how to solve this problem also. And she told him how to do it.

When the Tartar Prince received the rod and the answer, he could not deny it was correct and he was furious.

"I'll show them that no-one can get the better of me!" he cried out.

A few days later he marched with a large army and encamped near the capital and the royal castle.

As the people cowered in their houses horror-stricken, a spear came whistling through the air and hit the castle wall with such a thud that the old building shook as if it were an earthquake. The same old threat from the Tartar Prince was written on the spear: "Unless someone is able to pull this spear from the wall and throw it back again to my tent, I shall make an attack on your town, and destroy it, stone by stone, and kill all the inhabitants and marry the Princess."

The King could not get a wink of sleep. He called all the heroes in the country and all those who were born under a lucky star, so that they might try to pull out the spear. The one who succeeded was promised a great fortune. But it was all in vain, for no-one could move the spear so much as a hair's breadth.

More desperate than ever before the Princess went to the prisoner in the tower that night, and told him all that had happened.

"Dearest Princess," said the youth, "Trust me once again, and follow my advice. Have these loose stones blocked up again as if they had been in the wall all the time. Go then to your father and tell him that, in another dream, you saw that I was still alive and would be able to carry out the task."

This suggestion made the Princess more hopeful than she had been for days. When she had seen that the loose stones were put in their old places again, she went to her father and told him what she had learnt.

But the King only shook his head, and said despondently, "My dear child, I remember that boy well, but he must have died long ago, and his bones now lie moulding in the tower."

"But father, haven't I already given you many pieces of good advice through my dreams? Why then can't you try this one?"

The King decided it couldn't hurt to make an attempt and have a look inside the tower, though he was quite sure it would be in vain. In this hopeless situation he had, however, to try even the smallest chance.

The stones were taken out, and to their great amazement they saw the young man standing in front of them, strong and gallant. The King told him all about the Tartar Prince and the spear.

The young man fell on his knees before the King, and said, "Sire, you have nothing to fear, I shall carry out the task and rid the country of this terrible threat."

He was shown to the place where the spear had stuck in the wall. With both hands he grasped the spear and pulled it out with such force that the thick wall cracked from the battlements down to the foundations. Then he turned round and with equal strength threw the spear back again to the Tartar camp. It struck the Prince's own tent which tumbled down right over the head of the Prince himself.

When the spear came hurtling over his head the Prince grew quite pale. "Indeed a narrow escape," he thought, trembling from head to foot. This he certainly hadn't expected. Angrily he sent a messenger to the King that he was now willing to return home to his own castle and leave the King and his country alone on condition that the man who had carried out the deed was sent to him. He wanted to see the man who was his equal in strength, and learn if he was his equal in cunning as well.

When the youth heard this he offered himself at once to go to Tartary. He asked the King to let eleven young knights accompany him.

"Now it's my intention to defeat the Tartar's magic skill," he said. "I want to make these eleven knights exactly like myself. We must all be dressed in the same way, have the same armour, the same clothes and even cut our hair in the same style, and see if the Tartar Prince is able to pick out the one he wants to know."

"My dear young friend," answered the King, "you may ask anything of me. My armoury will stand at your disposal, and you may choose from it whatever suits you best. Besides that, I shall not only dub you a knight, but also make you the head of my noblest and finest warriors."

Before long a group of twelve young knights left the King's castle on their way to Tartary. All were of the same tall build equipped with equally splendid armour, with long gay plumes swinging from their glittering helmets. All were galloping along on shiny black steeds with the same fine trappings.

When they arrived at the Tartar Prince's castle they were made extremely welcome, and a feast was arranged in their honour with great pomp and splendour. But the Prince was quite puzzled, for whom should he address as the leader and welcome as the one he had invited? Who was his clever opponent who had dared to compete with him, the most feared and famous of all Princes? In vain he tried to find a sign to distinguish the leader from the rest of the group.

He was, however, too proud to show any sign of ignorance, so he decided to address them all in the same way even though this irritated him. He turned to his mother, who was a cunning

witch, for her help and advice.

She promised him to find out the wise hero with the strong arm, and with a cunning equal to their own. For this purpose she hid herself inside one of the hollow pillars supporting the ceiling in their guests' bedroom.

That night as they all lay in their beds talking about the many strange things they had seen in the foreign country, the witch spoke in a man's voice as if she were one of the knights: "What a splendid wine the Tartar Prince has got!"

"Do you call that a good wine?" retorted one of the knights, "It's mixed with blood."

The witch noticed from which bed the answer came. When she was sure that they had all fallen asleep, she stole out of her hiding place, went up to the bed and cut a piece off the forelock

of the sleeper. Then she went to her son and told him how she had marked the leader.

But next morning when the guests woke up their leader noticed that a piece had been cut from the forelock of his hair. To avoid being marked like this he cut a piece from the forelock of all his companions, so that they were all identical again.

At breakfast, the Prince was no wiser than the day before. He had to admit that this man was cleverer than he had thought.

Next night the witch stole into the guest bedroom again and stood hidden inside the pillar when the guests retired to sleep.

When they were all in bed and talking to each other as usual, a voice said, "What fine bread the Tartar Prince offers us."

"It isn't as good as you think, for it is salted with tears!" answered one of the knights.

And again the witch noticed from which bed the voice came. When they were all fast asleep, she stole out from her pillar and went up to the bed. This time she took some tar and made a tiny mark on the red plume of the helmet which stood beside the bed.

"No-one could possibly notice that unless they knew it was there," she thought triumphantly.

Early next morning she told her son about the marked plume on the helmet. When the twelve knights were mounting their horses for an early morning ride, the Tartar Prince was there to greet them.

"At last I've found you out!" he thought when he discovered a black spot on the red plume of the helmet of one of the knights. But turning round he found a similar spot on the red plumes of every helmet.

The Prince clenched his fists in anger. Once again his plans had been frustrated. "But the man hasn't yet escaped me!" he thought. "I'll make another try."

So for a third night the old witch was in her usual hiding place. When they were all lying in their beds talking, they once again heard the strange voice, "What a noble and gallant man the Tartar Prince is, isn't he?"

"Nothing very much to boast of," a voice answered, "He isn't even the real son of the late Tartar Prince."

The old witch gave a start of surprise where she stood hidden in the pillar. This man was indeed too clever for them all. He seemed to know even the private secrets of the Tartar court. It was absolutely necessary to find out who this man was. When the knights were asleep she stepped out of her pillar. She had noted from which bed the words came and decided this time to mark the bed itself. Even though it was the middle of the night she felt she had to fetch her son, so that he might come himself to the guest room and make away with this clever and dangerous man as soon as possible.

No sooner had she left the room than the young knight jumped out of bed. He woke up his friends and each one of them made a mark on their beds. Before they went back to sleep they put their swords beside them so as to have them at hand in case of need.

They had not been back in bed for very long, before the door opened, and the Tartar Prince stole up quietly to one of the beds. Noticing the mark he raised his sword intending to cut off the head of the man who lay there. As he did so, he turned his head, and saw a mark on the next bed as well, and then gradually he realised it was on all the other beds. He also noticed the swords that lay beside each one of the sleepers ready to grasp if something should happen to one of them. This made him change his mind, and he stole out again as quietly as he had come.

Next morning he greeted his guests with the same friendliness as usual. He now realised that nothing remained but to swallow his pride and anger, and ask the young knight to make himself known.

"I admit," he said, addressing the twelve knights, "that among you there is a greater master than myself. And I ask him to come up to me, so that I may learn to know the one who is my superior in strength and also in cunning."

The youth stepped forward and said, "It wasn't my intention to show myself as your superior. I only managed to carry out the tasks you put to us. And I'm also the one who for three nights has been marked by your mother."

"Well, young knight! Now you must tell us what you meant by saying that there was blood in the wine?"

"Let your butler come forward, he is the one to explain it," answered the young knight.

The butler came, shivering with fright, and said, "My Prince, when I heard that my brother was put in prison for a crime he hadn't committed, I got so nervous that I cut my finger when I drew the wine. Please spare my life, I assure you I couldn't help it."

The Prince, who wanted to show his guests what a good sovereign he was, told his butler that he had nothing to fear, and his brother should be released, the Prince himself would see to that.

"Well, it seems you were quite right there," he said turning to the young knight with suppressed anger. "But what do you mean by saying that the bread was salted with tears?"

"Let the baker's wife come, she may explain it," answered the youth. And the baker's wife came, quivering and sobbing.

"Oh, you mighty Lord of the Tartars! You let your men take my son away, and they hanged him before my very eyes. Why shouldn't I then cry all day, even when I have to bake your bread?"

The Prince had great difficulty in concealing his anger, but trying to show his guests that he wasn't the tyrant he seemed, he gave the baker's wife a golden coin, and told her she could leave.

"Again you were right," he said to the youth, "but now you must tell me what you meant by saying that I am not even the real son of the Tartars."

The young knight turned to the old witch: "You should be able to tell us the truth of this statement."

The old witch could do nothing except confess that it was really true. The Prince then lost control of himself. He flew into a passion and raising his sabre he rushed at the young man crying out, "I can't stand anyone getting the better of me! One of us has to die! Look out!"

At this the sabre flashed through the air, but the young knight had been equally quick. Like lightning his sword hit the Prince's sabre with such force that it flew out of his hand and the Prince tumbled and fell. This was the end of the cruel Tartar Prince, for the knight had run his sword through him.

No-one in the whole of Tartary regretted the death of the terrible tyrant Prince, except his mother. All the wise men in the country gathered to hold council to choose a new ruler. An old, venerable man rose and spoke, "May I suggest this young and gallant knight, who has fought so bravely against the Prince, should be his successor and rule over the Tartars? Has he not shown himself as his superior both in strength and wisdom? If you agree to this choice you may rise from your seats and beat with your sabres on your shields."

There was not one among them who hadn't admired the strength and courage of the young foreign knight. The deafening noise that followed showed that they gladly accepted the suggestion. So the youth became the new ruler of the Tartars.

Meanwhile the Princess sat in the castle waiting anxiously for her young knight to return. "Supposing he doesn't return at all?" she thought. "It is more than likely that the cruel Tartar Prince has killed him. Shall I ever see him alive again?" Day after day she wept and worried, longing for news.

One day, a message arrived at the royal castle to say that the Tartar Prince was on his way again, this time, however, with only a small bodyguard and eleven of the knights, who were returning home. He was coming to ask for the Princess's hand in marriage.

This was a bitter blow for the poor Princess. It meant of course, she thought, that her gallant knight and former prisoner was now dead. There was no longer anyone who could protect her and the country from this terrible enemy. Even the King felt sad for the valiant youth, and was most downhearted. He told his daughter that he could not see any other way out for her than to marry the Prince.

The Princess said nothing, she was too sad. She no longer cared what should become of her, since the man she loved was dead.

It was with a heavy heart that the King and his pretty daughter saw a party of knights approaching, carrying the hated Tartar Prince's banner. When the Prince dismounted and came up to greet the King and the Princess—they could hardly believe their eyes. This was their own young hero and former prisoner. Now the Princess no longer dreaded the day of her marriage!

The wedding was celebrated with great pomp and splendour; at the wedding-party the King turned to the bridegroom and said, "Well, my gallant Prince and dear son, I have a request for you. Would you now tell me your dream?"

"Yes my King and dear father! Now, I can tell you—I dreamt exactly everything that has happened to me since I ran from my father till this day. Had I told it earlier, it wouldn't have come true, or would it?"

# The Stubborn Shepherd
## A story from Hungary

LONG AGO there lived a strange shepherd. He didn't look at all odd or unusual, for he dressed like any other shepherd in his large slouch hat, his wide cloak slung over his shoulders, and his shepherd's crook in his hand. But the girls in the village called him "star-eyes" for he had eyes that glittered and twinkled like stars. They were eyes that could be so sparkling and gay that everyone else felt happy too. They were eyes that could be so strong and compelling that those who looked into them were held spellbound. All the boys called him "the stubborn shepherd" for he took no notice of what others said, but did exactly as he pleased. And once he had made up his mind about something, no-one could make him change it.

He had a particularly beautiful flute to whistle for his sheep, which he had made himself on the feast of Saint Vendelin, the patron saint of shepherds.

All day long he went out on the wide steppe, looking after his sheep. As evening came he blew a gay tune on his flute and the sheep came up immediately, so that he could drive them together with his shepherd's crook and count them. Every night after supper he went down to his local inn and there he entertained all his young friends with his flute, playing such merry tunes that everyone danced and sang.

The country in which the shepherd lived was ruled by a mighty King. Grim and stern, he insisted that his subjects should show him all the obedience and loyalty he expected. In particular, he was obsessed with the crazy idea that whenever he sneezed, every single person in his kingdom had to say *"prosit"* to him, which meant "Good Health to you!" As soon as he sneezed, a dozen courtiers would rush round the countryside saying *"prosit"* to everyone they saw. And every single subject, young and old, had to reply *"prosit"* or be reported to the King. People found this a terrible nuisance especially when the King had a cold.

One evening the shepherd, with some other young people, sat in the inn gaily chatting and laughing when a stranger entered.

*"Prosit"* the stranger called out to the customers. *"Prosit! Prosit!"* responded the people from everywhere, who recognised one of the King's men. All that is—except the shepherd. The stranger, who noticed that the shepherd sat silent, went up to him, put his hand on his shoulder and said, "Young man, don't you know that you have to say *'prosit'*?"

"What nonsense! Why should I?" cried the shepherd.

Rumours quickly reached the royal palace that there was a shepherd who refused to say *prosit* to the King. The King immediately sent for him, and he had to set out dressed as he was in his large slouch hat, and his wide cloak, carrying his shepherd's crook and his flute.

When the shepherd appeared before the King's throne, the

King looked very severely at him and said, "I have heard it said that you didn't say *prosit* to me. Will you now humbly say *prosit* to me at once!"

"*Prosit* to me," was the shepherd's prompt answer.

"No, you fool! To me, to me, of course!" snapped the King.

"Yes, to me, to me, of course," repeated the shepherd.

"You are a perfect idiot, *you* must say *prosit* to ME, to myself!" cried the King furiously patting himself on his chest.

"Yes, *prosit* to me, to myself," repeated the shepherd, patting himself slightly on his chest too.

This was too much for the King, he turned desperately to a courtier for help. This worthy nobleman went up to the shepherd and said to him, "You must say *prosit* to his Majesty at once or it may cost you your life."

"No, I won't say it unless I can marry the Princess," answered the shepherd.

The Princess was sitting on a smaller throne near her royal father, and was as pretty as a rose. She had enjoyed the whole conversation, and could not help laughing at the shepherd's last words. As a matter of fact she liked the keen young shepherd with the starry eyes better than any of the Princes who had been at her father's court to ask for her hand in marriage.

But the King did not laugh. This was indeed an impertinence that he could not tolerate.

"Guard!" he called out, "Seize this man, and throw him into the bear's cave. There the white bear will soon tear him into pieces."

The shepherd was thrown into the cave of the white bear that had not been given anything to eat for two days. The bear rushed on him at once, ready to tear him into a thousand pieces. Then the shepherd stared at the bear with his strange eyes and the bear crept slowly backwards into a corner of the cave with-

156

out daring to touch him. The shepherd went nearer and nearer towards the bear, gazing steadily at him, knowing that if he took his eyes away for a second the bear would at once tear him into pieces. At last the big white bear was so overcome by the big staring star-eyes that it tumbled down and fell fast asleep. The shepherd did not dare to sleep in case the bear woke up again.

The next morning when the guard came to see if there was anything left of the shepherd he found to his great surprise that the bear was sleeping peacefully in a corner of the cave, while the shepherd sat in the middle, wide awake, with not a hair on his head harmed.

The shepherd was brought before the King who was in a great temper.

"Now you have been near death," he said, "Won't you now say *prosit* to me?"

"No, I'm not afraid of a tenfold death. And I won't say it unless I can marry the Princess," was the shepherd's reply.

"Right then, you shall suffer the pains of a tenfold death!" called out the King. And he ordered the guard to throw the stubborn man to the giant boars, the fiercest animals of all the King's wild beasts.

Again the shepherd was seized by the guard, and they threw him into the cave where the fierce giant boars were kept. These wild beasts had not seen any food for four days and were terrible to set eyes on. With their long tusks ready for an attack they darted upon the poor young man. But just as he felt their hot breath on his face he pulled from his sleeve his flute, which was made on the day of Saint Vendelin, and began to play Saint Vendelin's own song.

At the sound of the flute the fierce animals shrank away and then slowly began to sway clumsily to and fro to the tune of

157

his flute.

It was a ridiculous sight and the shepherd had great difficulty in stifling his laughter and continuing to play. First he played slowly then he changed into more exciting dance music. The shepherd played on and on, until at last the beasts became so exhausted that they collapsed into an exhausted slumber. Then the shepherd burst out laughing, and he laughed and laughed until the guard next morning found him safe and sound in the cave roaring with laughter, the tears of mirth running down his cheeks. The wild beasts were lying fast asleep round him.

The guard had to take the shepherd out of the cave and lead him to the King. When the King saw him again still alive he could hardly believe his eyes.

"Now you have been near a tenfold death," said the King, "Won't you say *prosit* to me?"

"No, I'm not afraid of a hundredfold death, and I won't say it unless I can marry the Princess," answered the shepherd quietly.

"Then you shall indeed suffer a hundredfold death," said the King full of anger. "Guards! Seize the stubborn fool, and throw him into the scythe hole!" he ordered.

The guards dragged the unfortunate man to a prison kept for the worst criminals in the land. Here he was pushed into a dark cellar vault. The light from the open door behind him lit up the vault for a moment, revealing a deep, gaping hole in the middle of the floor. A hundred scythes glittered from the sides, their sharp edges turned towards him, ready. As he bent over he saw a tiny flickering flame deep down at the bottom.

"Why is there a light down there?" he said, turning to the guards who came forward to push him down. The guards stopped for a moment to answer this unexpected question.

"We always have a light down there," said one, "So as to

be sure that the victim we have thrown down really has reached the bottom."

This seemed a bit too grim to the shepherd.

"Could you please wait a moment?" he asked the guards. "Just give me a few minutes alone to think the matter over. Perhaps I may, after all, say *prosit* to the King."

"Yes, you stubborn fool, you may have a few minutes to think, but don't imagine there might be any chance to escape. We will be waiting right outside the door," was the answer. The guards left the vault and locked the door carefully behind them.

As soon as the door was locked and the shepherd was alone, he took his shepherd's crook, and stuck it upright in the ground, for there was no paved floor in the prison vault. Then he wound his scarf round it, and draped his wide cloak on top. Finally he placed his slouch hat where his head would be. Then he went to the door and called out to the guard. "Now I have considered the matter, and I still won't say *prosit* to the King." The shepherd pressed himself close to the wall behind the door.

As the door swung open he was completely hidden behind it, and the guards could only see a quiet figure bending over the edge of the scythe hole, in the same position as they had left the foolish shepherd a few minutes earlier. They gave him a push, and saw him falling right over the sharp edges of the scythes into the deep hole. Then the candlelight at the bottom went out and they were in no doubt that this was the very end of the stubborn shepherd. They went to the King to report that his order had been properly carried out.

Next morning the gaoler came into the vault with a torch to light a new candle for the scythe hole. Terrified he shrank back by the wall, his knees knocking and shaking, for he saw what he fearfully thought was the ghost of the shepherd walking towards him. Eventually the shepherd proved he was fully alive and once again he was brought before the King, who, like the gaoler, could hardly believe his eyes. When he was convinced that this troublesome man really was still alive, he shouted at him, "Now you have been near a hundredfold death, won't you say *prosit* to me!"

"No, I still won't say it unless I can marry the Princess," said the shepherd, steadfast as ever.

"Can this man be a mighty magician?" thought the King. "The wild beasts don't touch him and sharp steel doesn't hurt him. How on earth am I to get rid of him? Perhaps if I offer him a good fortune, he will say *prosit* to me for less than a marriage to my daughter," the King argued to himself.

So the King ordered his coach to the royal palace gate. He asked the shepherd to sit with him in the coach for a tour round the royal estates, and told his driver to take them to the silver wood.

After driving for about an hour they came to the most remarkable wood the shepherd had ever seen. It glittered and shimmered of pure silver. The needles of the firs and pines were silver and the leaves of the oaks and beeches. From the silver branches hung silver nuts and silver cones. Silver flowers grew in the fine silver grass, and even the spider's webs were spun of the daintiest silver thread.

"Do you see this wood?" asked the King. "This will all be yours if you say *prosit* to me."

Though the shepherd was overwhelmed by what he saw, he only said again, "I won't say it unless I can marry the Princess." The King looked completely baffled at the stubborn man, he couldn't believe this was possible. And he told the driver to continue to the golden palace.

They came after a while to a palace made of white marble

and pure gold. Its golden pillars and golden roof shimmered so that the shepherd had to shut his eyes to protect them from the bright glare.

"This golden palace shall I give to you," said the King, "as well as the silver wood, if only you will say *prosit* to me."

But the shepherd said as before, "I won't say it unless I can marry the Princess."

The King was at a loss. He had just one more precious possession which surpassed everything else he owned and even that he was prepared to offer. "Drive on to the diamond pond!" he called out desperately to the driver.

When they reached the pond the shepherd could only blink in amazement, wondering if he was dreaming. The pond was full of thousands and thousands of diamonds which flashed and flamed in the sunlight like clusters of tiny rainbows.

"Look carefully at his diamond pond," said the King. "For the pond, the silver wood, and the golden palace will all be yours, if you say *prosit* to me. Think for a few moments before your answer, consider what this will really mean to you."

The shepherd shut his eyes so he would not be confused by the dazzling sight, and said firmly as before, "I won't say it unless I can marry the Princess."

Then the King realised that nothing on earth could make this stubborn man change his mind. As a King he could not of course leave the matter at that, the shepherd simply *had* to say *prosit* to him. So the King said, "Well, you may marry my daughter, but then you really must say *prosit* to me."

"Oh yes, then of course! Why shouldn't I *then* say *prosit?* It will be quite natural then and I shall say it quite easily and willingly." The King was at last satisfied with this agreement.

Splendid wedding feasts were arranged so that all the people in the country could take part in them. Most splendid of all, though, were the banquets and balls at the royal palace, where hundreds of guests were invited and the most famous gipsy bands played their violins.

All the guests were sitting down for their meal and the large pig's head was served. Suddenly the smell of the strong horse-radish which garnished the dish tickled and irritated the royal nose. The King went pink, gasped and gave a most *enormous* sneeze.

"*Prosit,* your Majesty!" cried out the shepherd before anyone else had time to say anything.

The King was so pleased that he proclaimed the shepherd King of half his Kingdom. The shepherd became a very wise and good King who never asked his people to do anything for him against their own free will.

# The Little Mermaid
*A story from Denmark, by Hans Andersen*

FAR OUT TO SEA, where the water is as clear as crystal and blue as an evening summer sky, it is so deep that an anchor cannot reach the bottom. You might think that the sea bed is flat and only covered with fine white sand, but this is not true at all. There are high hills and deep valleys covered with wonderful corals and plants whose stems are thick with long leaves swinging to and fro to the movements of the water. There are sea flowers, shimmering in many colours which open and close their petals like daisies. Instead of birds in those lovely sea-gardens, there are fishes of all sizes and colours. Some have fins which they swing like birdwings as they dart around the plants, and they look just like birds.

Where the sea is deepest stands the palace of the mighty Sea-King, King of all the sea-people, the mermaids and the mermen. His palace is magnificent. It has walls of coral, high windows of the clearest amber, and a roof of shimmering mother-of-pearl. Instead of furniture he has huge gleaming mussel-shells, and every one is studded with pearls.

The Sea-King had six little Princesses, who were beautiful with long golden hair; they had no legs or feet but a little silver fish-tail so that they could swim easily and dart about in the water. The prettiest of them all was the youngest Princess. Her cheeks were like rose-petals, her hair hung right down to the tip of her tail, and her slender little body slipped through the water faster than anyone else.

All day long the little Princesses played in their lovely garden. They played with crabs, sea-stars and lobsters, and they taught the fishes to swim up and eat out of their hands.

Sometimes, when they grew tired of playing in their wonderful garden, they made little tours together to other places. Often they discovered things from a wrecked ship which had sailed high up over their heads on the surface of the sea; strange and wonderful things which made them long to know more of the world outside their father's kingdom.

But the youngest Princess pondered over these things much more than her elder sisters. She liked to gather the little bits and pieces and hide them in a secret place in the garden, where she could sit and dream of the world above. But no mermaid could ever leave the sea, and the Princesses were not even allowed to float up to the surface before they were fifteen years old. As the little Princess was the youngest she had to wait for a long, long time yet.

One day her eldest sister was allowed to float up to the surface. She had a hundred tales to tell her younger sisters when she came home again. She told them of the towns and wonderful buildings which she could see on the shore beside the sea, and human creatures on two clumsy legs slowly walking about, and small children playing in the sand on the beach. They had strange, shrill voices, not like the mermaids who sang so sweetly that even the birds stopped their music to listen. Each year another of the sisters went up to the surface, and each one had another tale to tell about what she had seen. One told of the blue sky and the seabirds which darted down to feed on the fish, or folded their wings and rocked on top of the waves. Another told of dark woods with high trees and green fields. Sometimes they spoke of glittering sunshine on smooth water and how it changed at sunset when the water glimmered red and gold, or how the water could be lashed into huge waves crested with foam by fierce, terrible storms. They would tell of the glittering icebergs that floated on frozen seas, and of snow that came from the chalky sky.

The story the little Princess liked to hear best of all was about the big ships that set their high, white sails to the wind and sailed so fast over the water.

On many evenings the five sisters joined hands and rose to the surface while their little sister waited longingly for the day to come when she could join them. At last that day arrived, and the Sea-King held a great party. The Palace was lit by a thousand mussel-shells with sea-fire and the Princesses wore strings of pearls round their slender necks and crowns of pearls on their long golden hair.

Next morning all six sisters joined hands, and rose as lightly as bubbles to the surface of the sea. Now the little Princess could at last enjoy the bright shining sun and breathe the fresh air. They rocked on the tops of the waves and sang their lovely sweet voices, but clearer and sweeter than the other sisters sang the little mermaid who saw for the first time everything she had longed for.

Her sisters were soon tired and went home, but their little sister swam about alone all day. When the sun sank and it grew dark the Princess swam close to a big, fine ship and looked in

165

at the lighted windows. She saw people feasting and dancing in honour of the Prince on board. Nobody could see the little mermaid peeping in at the window.

Before long a storm blew up and the waves lashed across the deck of the ship. The sailors struggled to keep it upright, but the sea was too fierce. A sudden tremendous wave smashed the side of the ship and it sank down to the bottom of the sea.

The Prince swam bravely for a time, until, exhausted, he could not struggle any longer. Then the little mermaid swam up to him and taking his heavy weight in her arms she struggled bravely to help him to the shore. Looking up she saw a magnificent palace overlooking the sea, with a flight of white marble steps leading down to the sandy beach. It was here that she carefully laid him down, wishing desperately that she could have taken him to her father's palace. But she knew that men cannot live in the sea as fishes and mermaids can.

She hid behind some rocks to see what would happen to the handsome Prince. After a few minutes a young woman came slowly down the steps to the sea and stared in astonishment when she discovered the young man lying on the sands. She bent over him to make certain that he was not dead, and when he moved and looked up at her, she called for help. People came running out to join her and between them they carried the Prince inside the palace.

For a while the little mermaid sat staring at the porch into which her Prince had disappeared. "Shall I ever see him again?" she wondered miserably. With a deep sigh she dived into the water and swam to her father's palace.

The little mermaid now became more quiet and thoughtful than before. While her sisters sang or sat on the rocks combing their long golden hair, or darted about in the water, she sat sadly dreaming. Many times she swam to the beach where she

had left the Prince and looked longingly at the large palace, hoping to catch a glimpse of him, but he never appeared again.

At last she could not bear it any longer and told her sisters about her adventure, begging them to help her find out where the Prince lived. With the help of their many friends they managed to discover where his kingdom was, and they swam there with their little sister. After that she often swam all by herself, right to the shore, as far as she dared, and sat gazing at his palace. One day she was overjoyed to see him going aboard a new ship, she swam beside it peeping in through the portholes, and was happy to see him healthy and handsome as before. At other times she swam round the fishermen's boats in his harbour and heard how proudly they spoke about their noble young Prince, and she was glad she had saved his life when he was floating unconscious on the waves.

During her visits to the shore, she grew to like humans more and more, and wished that she could go up amongst them, and learn more about the world. There were so many questions about the "upper world" as she and her sisters used to call it, that she wanted to know about, but her sisters could tell her very little.

Now, there lived a wise old mermaid in her father's palace who knew all about the upper world, and the little princess decided to call on her to ask her some of the questions she had been worrying about.

"If a man from the higher world falls into the water, can he live for ever here with us? Can we live for ever down here in our world?"

"No, my dear," the old mermaid answered. "He must die, and so must we. But it will be quite different for him. He has a much shorter life, but we can live here for more than three hundred years. Look at me, I am now more than two hundred.

But when we end our lives here, we become foam on the waves, and we can never have any life again.

"The people of the upper world have a much shorter life, but they have a soul which lives for ever, even after their bodies have turned to dust. It floats up through the clear blue sky right up to the stars. Just as we can rise to the surface of the sea and get a glimpse of their countries above us, they can fly up to lovely unknown lands which we can never reach."

"Why haven't we got an immortal soul like that?" asked the little Princess, full of sorrow. "I should gladly give away a hundred years of my life to live for a single day among the people in the world above, and then afterwards reach their heaven."

"Forget that idea at once! Believe me, we are much better off down here. We lead an easier life without cares and sorrows."

"But is there nothing I can do to get a life up there and gain an immortal soul?"

"No, nothing, little Princess!" the old mermaid answered, "unless you can find a man among the people up there who would love you so much that you became dearer to him than his father and mother. If he took you to church and let a clergyman bless you as his married wife, then part of his soul would flow into your body and you would have a share of human happiness. But I tell you this can never happen to you, because your fishtail, which we think is beautiful, they consider ugly, and use two props called legs for walking with."

The little mermaid looked sadly down at her shiny fishtail and sighed. "Don't look so sad little Princess. Tonight your father is arranging a ball, and you must forget your dreams and enjoy yourself."

The large ballroom was made of thick, clear crystal and had been decorated in fantastic splendour. Round the walls hundreds of mussel-shells were placed with glowing flames in different colours. They lit up the large ballroom and shone through the crystal water round it so that all the fishes swimming round the palace caught the shimmering light and turned silver and gold.

In the large hall mermaids and mermen sang and danced to their own beautiful songs. Their songs surpassed anything that we mortals have ever heard, but the little mermaid who was the King's youngest daughter sang more beautifully than anyone. At first she was happy and enjoyed the ball like the others, but soon she began to think of the handsome young Prince who had an immortal soul and of herself who had none. He, whom she loved more than father and mother, might even now be sailing in a boat over her head. "I wish that one day he would take my hand in his, and make me his wedded wife," she said longingly to herself.

While everybody was so busy enjoying themselves she left her father's palace unnoticed and swam away. She had made up her mind to ask the old Sea-Witch to help her. She swam away through the beautiful garden and soon left it far behind. At last she came to a dreary place where no sea-flowers grew, no pretty shells or starfish lay on the path and the water swirled in pools over grey, muddy sand. Large pale eels like snakes wriggled about, ugly cuttlefish swam round viciously, and polyps, half animal, half plant, flung out their shiny branch-arms, as if they wanted to hurt her.

Just as a large cuttlefish was on the point of catching her with one of its long tentacles, she managed to slip into a dark cave and escape. This was the home of the old Sea-Witch, who came hobbling towards the Princess when she saw her entering.

"I know what you have come for, you silly Princess," she said, "You want to have legs and feet instead of your pretty tail.

I can't think why you should want to be so ugly and walk on two stick-like legs as men do."

"Can you give them to me?" asked the little mermaid.

"Oh yes, I certainly can do that," answered the old witch. "Wait a little, and I will mix you a strong drink which will burn like fire, but it will turn your tail into legs and feet, with which you will be able to dance better than anyone on land."

Then the witch went into a chamber where she kept all kinds of mysterious things, opened bottles and boxes and put a mixture into a cauldron. Then she cut open her finger and let a few drops of her own blood drop into it. She put the cauldron on the fire to boil, and after a while she came out to the Princess with a bottle in her hand.

"Swim ashore and drink this before the sun rises and you will get what you wish. Your tail will split into two pretty little legs, but it will hurt like the stab of a sharp sword. And each time you put your dainty feet on the ground, it will be like walking on a bed of nails. Never again will you become a mermaid, or dive down and visit your father or your sisters. And if you cannot win the Prince's love so that he makes you his dear wife, you will never have an immortal soul. The day he weds another, your heart will break and you will become just a speck of foam on the sea. Are you willing to suffer this?"

"Yes, I'm willing," gasped the Princess and she took the bottle from the witch, holding out her fine long pearl necklace in payment for it. But the Sea-Witch shook her head.

"No, no, my dear," she croaked, "I must be paid far more than that. This is a very rare mixture, and I have given my own blood to it. The best gift you have I demand for my precious drink. You must give me your little red tongue in exchange."

"If I lose my voice what would then be left to me?" asked

the Princess, very distressed.

"You have your beautiful slender body, and your graceful movements, and your large, beautiful expressive eyes. They are enough to charm any man."

"Very well," whispered the little mermaid and gave her tongue to get her wish, so that she could neither sing nor speak. When she had recovered from the pain, she was ready to leave the cave.

"Look out," the witch said, "Take a few drops from the bottle and drop them on the cuttlefishes and the polyps which guard my cave, and they won't harm you."

But there was no need to use the costly contents of the bottle which the Princess held in front of her, for as soon as those dreadful creatures of the sea caught sight of the liquid in the Princess's hand, they shrank away in fear. The Princess went back to her father's palace to have a last look at her dear sisters and her old father, whom she was leaving for ever in the palace at the bottom of the sea. She threw them a thousand kisses as they lay sleeping, and then swam to the shore by the young Prince's palace. In the moonlight she drank the burning liquid from the bottle, and felt a sharp pain stab through her body. She fell unconscious on the sand.

When she opened her eyes again, she saw her Prince bending over her. Looking down at her tail she discovered that it had gone, and in its place she had two beautiful, slender legs and perfectly-shaped little feet, but she was quite naked so she wrapped herself in her long, thick golden hair. The Prince asked who she was and where she came from, but the little mermaid could only look sweetly at him with her large sad eyes, unable to say anything. So the Prince took her by the hand and led her into his palace, and bid her welcome to his country and his home.

How glad she felt to be near him! Though every step she took sent sharp pains through her tiny feet, and she could not tell him how much she loved him nor how she had saved his life. The Prince ordered costly dresses to be made for her, and his court loved and admired her as the most beautiful of them all. She sat beside the Prince while the Court sang and danced before the Royal Family. There was one who sang better than the others and was much admired for her fine voice. The little mermaid knew she had sung far more beautifully and thought sadly to herself, "If only they knew that I have given away my voice for ever just to be here with the Prince."

When lovely melodies were played and there was dancing, the beautiful little mermaid lifted her slender arms and glided out on tiptoe over the floor, dancing as lightly as a snowflake on her slender feet. Nobody knew the agony she suffered, as if she were treading on sharp knives everytime her feet touched the floor. They sat enchanted, dazzled by the beauty of her movements and the charm of her slender body and expressive eyes.

The Prince was delighted and called her his little foundling insisting she should always be near him. Even when he was out hunting he let her follow him on horseback through the fresh green woods, which she enjoyed because her feet did not pain her. If they climbed the hills together her dainty feet seemed almost raw, but she showed no sign of what she suffered: she was so happy to be with him, wherever he went.

At night when everybody in the large palace was asleep, she stole out and went to the sea-shore to cool her aching feet. She looked out over the water and thought of her dear sisters, deep down in her father's palace at the bottom of the sea.

Every day that passed the Prince grew more and more fond of his little foundling. But to make her his wife never occurred to him. He liked her as a friend, a dear, good child. She realised that she never could hope for an immortal soul, but she could not love him any less, even though she knew that if he married another she would become a speck of foam on the sea.

"You are so dear to me," the Prince told her, "because you remind me of a beautiful girl who saved me once, when I was drowning, and whom I have never seen again." The mermaid wondered if he really meant her, or the girl who found him on the sand outside her home. Never had she missed her voice more than now, when she longed to tell him what had happened that day in the storm. But alas, she could not say a word.

One day the Prince asked her to come with him in his fine new boat, to sail to a neighbouring country. "Are you afraid of the sea, little foundling?" he asked, and he told her about the waves tipped with white foam in a storm, of smooth glittering water on a calm summer day, of weird fishes in the deep, and about the world under the water of which his divers had told him. And her eyes looked so sadly at him while her mouth smiled, for how could he guess that she knew much more about that world than he could ever imagine?

The Prince sailed to the foreign country where the King had a lovely daughter. The little mermaid longed to see her for she had heard so much of her beauty. When she did she had to admit to herself that this Princess was indeed very charming.

The Prince told her how wonderful the Princess was. "Now I know who I am going to marry," he said, "and you my little foundling will be the first to hear my secret, because you are my dearest friend. You see, it was this Princess who once saved my life when I was ship-wrecked on these very shores, and brought me to her home."

The little mermaid felt as if her heart would break, but she couldn't tell him how mistaken he was. She knew that on his wedding day, she must die and become white foam on the waves of the sea.

The night after the magnificent wedding feast, the little mermaid stood at the bulwark of the boat looking out over the sea. Suddenly, she saw on the water near the boat the pale faces of her five sisters, and even her old father was with them. They no longer had their long golden hair floating behind them on the water as they came swimming towards her.

"Dear, dear sister, come back to us, we are so sad without you. Hurry before the sun rises! We want to save you. Look, we have been to the Sea-Witch and she has given us this sharp knife, for which we have paid with our long golden hair. Tonight, when the Prince is asleep, you must go to him and stab the knife into his heart. If you do this you will once more turn into a mermaid, and sing and dive with us as before."

Reluctantly she took the knife, and went slowly to the cabin where the Prince was sleeping. She stooped over his bed, and she heard how he whispered the name of his beautiful bride. The knife trembled in her hand and with a sob she threw it far out into the sea through the open cabin window. Then she turned once more to give the sleeping Prince a last glance.

She stood at the bulwark and looked out at the sea, hearing her sisters' sad voices in the distance. Then she sprang into the water, feeling her body melt into foam as she touched the waves.

Just then the sun rose, and as its gentle rays fell on the foam, the little mermaid saw hundreds of tiny transparent fairies dancing in the air. She realised that she, too, had a tiny body like theirs, which rose out of the foam towards them.

"No one can see us," they sang softly, "but we have plenty to do. We carry the scent of the flowers to heal the sick and comfort poor people, and we blow the pollen from flower to flower. We make a mild breeze to blow the ships on their way, and cool the parched, hot countries on the earth."

That was what became of the sweet little mermaid, and she dances in the sunshine with the other fairies. The handsome Prince and his beautiful bride have long been forgotten, but the story of the faithful little mermaid will always be remembered, for the people in the story-teller's country loved her so much that they made a pretty statue of her, and she sits on a rock by the sea looking down into the water, as if she was looking for her sisters.

# The Terrible Witch Pudullia
## A story from Italy

THERE WAS GREAT EXCITEMENT in the little kingdom of
Padonia for the King's three beautiful daughters Fabiella,
Vesta and Rita were all to be married on the same day, and
there was going to be the most magnificent wedding anyone
had ever seen.

A short while before, three young and valiant knights came
to the court of Padonia and asked the King for the Princesses'
hands in marriage. When the King learnt that they were the
three sons of the mighty King of Velprato, the Princes Rollo,
Rillo and Rallo, he had no objections to make, on the contrary,
he was more than happy to have suddenly found suitable
husbands for all of his daughters.

Preparations were immediately started for a wedding to be
celebrated with all the pomp and splendour of which the little
kingdom was capable.

The long-awaited day came at last, and everywhere people
were busy with the last minute preparations for the great

celebration. In the parks round the royal palace gay, coloured lanterns were put up, and hundreds of fountains were built to send glittering cascades high into the air. The royal kitchen was filled with cooks and scullions busily putting the final finishing touches to the rich, tasty dishes, and giving the large wedding cakes their last beautiful decorations. Even the noble guests from foreign countries were busy dressing in silk and velvet with their long purple robes and putting their crowns on their heads. They knew that they had to look their very best for the celebrations so they had no time left for anything else.

Everyone was so busy that they completely forgot about two children, who for the first time in their lives were left to do as they pleased. They were the young Prince Tittone, a twelve-year old boy, the only son of the King of Padonia, and heir to the throne, and the little Princess Minella, the ten-year-old sister of the three bridegrooms. The two royal children now had a wonderful time together playing in the large parks around the palace.

"Let's play hide and seek!" suggested Prince Tittone.

"Oh yes, my favourite game," cried little Minella. "Look, take my silver pipe, and whistle with it when you are ready to start looking for me."

"Then you shall have my silver horn. When you have hidden somewhere just blow a note, so that I shall know in what direction I must look for you," said Tittone handing her a little silver horn which he had once got as a christening gift.

However cleverly they hid themselves among rose-bushes or under dense cypress branches they had had no difficulty in finding each other when they heard the silver horn or the silver pipe. They laughed and enjoyed themselves all day long and found such pleasure in each other's company that they decided to get married as soon as they were old enough.

When the afternoon came they were called indoors to get ready for the great wedding ceremonial in the large throne hall. As they entered, the two children saw that the whole court was already gathered and all the royal guests had taken their seats. Prince Rollo stood beside Princess Fabiella, Prince Rillo beside Princess Vesta, and Prince Rallo beside Princess Rita. Soon young Prince Tittone stood beside Princess Minella, but they stood a little apart from the others, for they were not going to be married that day.

Everybody stood there solemnly looking at each other as if they were waiting for something. The cardinal, who was going to perform the wedding-ceremony, opened the large prayer book, glanced towards the door, and shut the book again. The King and Queen of Padonia looked nervously at each other, and the magnificence of their ermine robes and golden crowns could not conceal their anxiety.

"What *is* the matter?" "What *are* they waiting for?" The whispers went from one to another, all round the large hall. Little Minella whispered to Tittone, "Is there anything wrong? Why don't they start?"

"Well, you see, it's because of my aunt, Princess Pudullia," Tittone whispered back, as soft as a mouse. "She might be a Princess, but she is also an ugly, terrible witch. We dare not begin this ceremony until she arrives. She is awfully touchy, you know, and she may do something horrible if we start before she is here."

"How thrilling, to see a real witch!" answered Minella enthusiastically, but in a very low voice.

"Hush! You don't know what you are talking about!" retorted Tittone whispering. "Once I told her I *thought* she had got a pimple on her nose—although in fact she has hundreds—and she turned my nose round, so that I had to walk about with an upside-down nose for a whole year. Whatever you do, don't say anything about her looks, however disgusting you may find her," warned Tittone.

The Princesses Fabiella, Vesta and Rita also took the opportunity to warn their bridegrooms not to make any remarks about their Aunt Pudullia's appearance.

Suddenly all the murmuring and whispering ceased, and everyone was still, so still that you could hear a pin drop. The door opened and in came Princess Pudullia. She was magnificently dressed in golden silk brocade with a purple velvet robe hanging from her shoulders, but in spite of this splendour she still looked the terrible witch she actually was. She held her large head proudly erect on her broad shoulders, for she had hardly any neck. In the middle of her haggard face loomed a nose, long and pointed like the beak of a bird. Her eyes were rather like those of a fish, and her hands with their long nails were more like the claws of a wild beast than a human hand. One of these claw-like hands was clenched round a black stick on which she leaned as she solemnly walked across the hall to her seat. Everyone shuddered at the awful sight of the witch, but not a sound was uttered.

As she passed the three bridal couples, in spite of the warnings they had had, the bridegrooms suddenly could not restrain the disgust they felt for this terrible witch.

"Ugh! She looks like a wild beast!" whispered Prince Rollo so low that the words were hardly audible even to Princess Fabiella.

"Ugh! She looks like a bird!" whispered Prince Rillo.

"Ugh! She looks like a fish!" whispered Prince Rallo.

Minella was no more able to suppress her feelings than her elder brothers.

"She really *does* look like a witch!" She whispered to Tittone.

Though all four of them had whispered in voices so low that they were like soft sighs Pudullia stopped and turned her head, for she had excellent hearing, and had heard every word they had whispered.

With a face distorted in fury she turned to Prince Rollo and screamed "Well, Prince Rollo, if you think I look like a wild beast, you can feel what it's like to be one yourself," and pointing to him with her black stick she mumbled some secret words. Instantly Prince Rollo disappeared, and in his place a wild boar ran about in the hall.

People grew stiff with horror and dismay, but Pudullia took no notice of anyone and went up to the second Prince. Again she raised her black stick and said "And you, Prince Rillo, say that I look like a bird. As punishment for that you shall henceforth be a bird yourself!" She pointed to him muttering her magic words. The next moment Prince Rillo was gone and a large eagle circled round the hall.

Screams of horror and anguish were heard again from everyone. The poor King and Queen of Velprato were stricken dumb by the fearful things that happened to their sons. But indifferent to all the anguish and havoc she had caused, Pudullia went on to Prince Rallo. "You, Prince Rallo, think that I look like a fish, well, as punishment *you* shall now be a fish!" And saying this she pointed to him with her stick murmuring as before. Prince Rallo disappeared and where he had stood there wriggled a big shark on the floor. Just as the cries of pity and dismay reached their peak, a large tidal-wave came rolling up to the palace gate and a strong wind blew open the door of the throne hall so that the wave swept in. As it rolled back again it swept the shark out into the sea. At the same time the wild boar ran out into the forest and the eagle was able to fly into the open air where it soared high up in the sky.

The terrible witch Pudullia, however, had not yet finished all the havoc she intended. "And you, Princess Minella," she said, reaching out her stick again, "So you think I look like a real witch. Well, for your punishment you shall learn to know me a little closer!" As she said this she sat astride her black stick, and seizing Minella's arm pulled her on to the stick in front of her. She whistled harshly through her fingers, and the stick at once rose up in the air and flew out through an open window with both of them.

Then everyone who had been rooted terror-stricken to their places broke out in loud cries of grief. The King and Queen of Velprato, who had now lost all their children, could not be comforted, and the three Princesses, Prince Tittone and the King and Queen of Padonia mourned with them.

The wedding feast, which had started in such splendour, now ended in horror and grief, and all the guests trailed sadly back to their homes.

Some days later three strange messages arrived for the King of Padonia. Just as the King was leaving his palace one morning, a fox came running right up the main steps to the porch and dropped a letter at the King's feet, then the fox disappeared as suddenly as it had come. Later, as the King was walking in the park, a pigeon flew low over his head and dropped a letter just in front of him. The third message came to the King in the strangest way of all. As he was going to dinner his chief cook asked for an audience. He handed the King a message which had been found inside the river-trout which the cook had bought that very morning.

All three messages were the same:

"We three former Princes, Rollo, Rillo, and Rallo, have been rulers over people. Now we have become rulers over animals. Each of us has part of the animal world to rule over. The wild boar over the four-legged animals, the eagle over the birds, and the shark over the fish, and we live in splendid palaces. As we have been engaged to the three Princesses of Padonia we herewith claim our brides, and we warn you that if you refuse us our rights you shall regret it.

"If you are willing to keep your promise and give us the Princesses as wives you may hoist a white flag on your palace as a signal, and we shall come within three days to fetch our brides."

No wonder these messages upset the King. There couldn't, of course, be any question of giving away his beautiful daughters as wives to wild beasts, birds and fishes. So there wasn't any white flag to be seen on the royal palace on that day nor the next. When three days had passed, and still no white flag had been hoisted, some dreadful plagues came over the country of Padonia. Rabbits and rats crept out of the woods in huge hordes, eating up the crops in the fields and the vegetables in the gardens. Tens of thousands of birds came like dense clouds darkening the sky, sparrows, crows and magpies; they all swooped down on the trees in the orchards eating up the fruits. But this wasn't all, for in the sea all kinds of strange monsters and huge fishes rose up to the surface stirring the water so that the waves rose as high as houses and one ship after the other became wrecked in the rough seas off the coast.

Then the King understood that there was nothing else to be done but to give in and hoist the white flag.

Once again a wedding had to be arranged, and the three Princesses had to be dressed in their bridal gowns with crowns on their heads. The whole court gathered again in the throne hall and the cardinal stood ready with the service book open in front of him. Only the three bridegrooms had not yet arrived, and there were many who secretly hoped they wouldn't appear at all.

But suddenly the door flung open and with a terrible clatter the wild boar galloped into the hall and placed himself beside Princess Fabiella. At the same time the eagle came flying in and swooped down beside Princess Vesta. A lot of dull thumps were heard followed by heavy shuffling, and in came four seals, balancing a huge tub on their heads with the greatest difficulty, as they slithered forward. They lowered the tub to the floor beside Princess Rita, and the sharp fin of the shark could be seen swimming around inside.

Now the cardinal could at last begin reading the marriage service from his large prayer book and this strange wedding-ceremony could take place. What a sad wedding it was, for no one showed the slightest sympathy with the three bridegrooms, except Prince Tittone. He went round to each one of them to say some words of consolation. He patted the wild boar on his back and said, "You may rest assured, dear brother-in-law, that when I'm grown-up I shall set out to kill that terrible witch Pudullia, find your sister and revenge the three of you."

And the wild boar answered, "If you are able to make an end to that wicked witch who has disappeared with our sister and turned us into wild beasts, you will also deliver us from her witchcraft."

Then Tittone went to the eagle and the shark and said the same thing to them. All of them seemed to appreciate the keen young boy's readiness to deliver them from the witch, and they promised to do what they could to help him.

"Will you pull out three hairs from my coat," said the wild boar, "and take good care of them. If you need my help you have only to let them fall to the ground and stamp on them calling out: 'This way! Brother Boar!' and I shall immediately be at your side."

The eagle told Tittone to take three feathers from his wings and let them fly in the air, crying: "This way! Brother Eagle!" Then the eagle would come at once to his aid. The shark said if he would pull out three scales from his tail-fin and rub them in his hand shouting out: "This way! Brother Shark!" he would at once be there to help him.

Tittone took all the things he was offered and placed them carefully into a little silver box which he put into his pocket, promising to carry it about with him at all times.

Then the three strange, newly-married couples said farewell to their parents and parents-in-law, and went to their new homes. From that day they were surrounded by silence, and nothing was heard of them for many years. As for the poor little Princess Minella, no one knew what had become of her.

Tittone, however, could not forget her. Every day he thought of her and wondered what the wicked witch might have done to her. Many times he went to his father asking if it wasn't yet time for him to set out into the world and try to deliver his three brothers-in-law and get rid of that awful witch Pudullia. But always his father made the same excuse:

"You are not yet old enough or strong enough for such a dangerous task. Wait until you are eighteen and then we'll speak about it."

The old King secretly hoped that by that time his son and heir would have forgotten all about this daring adventure.

But the years went by, and at last Tittone's eighteenth birthday was celebrated. Once again Tittone stood in front of his father and asked him for permission to set out and find that terrible witch Pudullia.

Now the King could not find any reasonable excuse to refuse, for the young Prince in front of him had grown up into a fine splendid youth, strong as a lion and agile as a panther. He was indeed no longer a child. The King realised that he must now give in to his demand, and so he gave him his blessing.

The young Prince equipped himself with everything he might need on his long and daring journey. The last thing he did, before he mounted his horse, was to make sure that the things he valued most, Princess Minella's silver pipe and the little silver box with his brothers-in-law's hairs, feathers and scales, were safe in his pocket.

Then he took a long and sad farewell of his parents and set off. He passed one kingdom after another without finding the faintest trace of his Aunt Pudullia. He had no idea in what direction he should ride to find her dreaded castle. Sometimes he took out the little silver pipe Minella had given him and blew a few notes. He hoped that she might perhaps chance to hear it, if she was anywhere within reach of the sound, and then she would answer with the silver horn he had given to her. But he never heard even one faint tone from a silver horn in response. Not a single person of all those he asked had ever heard of the terrible witch Pudullia.

He had now been searching for his aunt for a whole year and felt quite desperate and discouraged. He decided he had better give up all hope of ever finding her and return home, though it was with a heavy heart he made this decision. Even that seemed easier to say than to do, for he had come to a vast wilderness in which he had lost his way and didn't know how to get out of it.

When he finally saw high mountains in the far distance he spurred on his horse and rode towards them and up the steep ridges trying to reach the peak of one mountain to get a good view of the countryside so he could discover the best way out of the wilderness. It was no easy matter reaching the top on horseback, and in the end he had to dismount and lead the horse while he struggled along on foot. But at last he stood on the summit. He had an excellent view, but all he could see was high cliffs and forests with here and there the glitter of a tiny lake among the mountains.

He felt completely alone in an uninhabited world and trying not to feel too miserable, he took out his little pipe and whistled to cheer himself up. The notes echoed all over the countryside for from the top of the mountain he had a wide range. And Tittone blew once again, and again it echoed round about, and he blew a third time. Did he dream, was it only a mocking echo, or did he really hear a signal from the horn he had given Minella? He blew again, and again the signal of a horn answered. Now he no longer hesitated which direction to take. He climbed down the mountain, jumped on his horse and set off as fast as he could through the wilderness towards the sound of the horn-signals, just as he had done as a child when he played hide and seek with Minella.

He rode on, with the trees gradually becoming less dense and then, suddenly, his horse stopped on the shores of a small lake. In the middle of the lake there was an island, and in the middle of the island rose a gloomy castle with thick, grey stone walls and high towers. In an open window in one of the towers he saw a beautiful young girl with a silver horn in her hand. Though Tittone did not recognize her, he cried out excitedly,

"Can you *really* be Minella?"

"Yes, yes, and you are surely Tittone?" she shouted back joyfully. But soon her joy changed to fear, and she became grave and sad.

"Please be careful. You can't possibly stay here any longer. As soon as the wicked Pudullia catches sight of you, she will have her revenge with all the evil spells she knows, and you will be completely destroyed. Although she is asleep now, she could

wake up any minute. Please, try and escape while there is still time."

"She's still asleep? That's marvellous. I shall come at once and finish that terrible monster off for ever!"

In spite of Minella's warnings he drove his horse down into the water and swam with him to the little island. Then the young Prince stood dripping wet, but happy, under Minella's window.

"Now, my dear, you must let me in, whether you want to or not, and show me where that monster is, so that I can give her what she deserves."

Minella pleaded with him again and warned him how dangerous it would be if Pudullia should wake up. "She will certainly not let you off with being an animal as she did my brothers."

"Do you think that after I've been searching for her a whole year now, I shall run away as soon as I've found her?"

Minella could do nothing but show Tittone into Pudullia's bedroom. They entered the room on tiptoe, trying desperately not to waken the old witch. There she lay in a high four-poster, with the costly curtains pulled slightly apart, and the whole bed shook with her loud snores.

"You must cut off her head in one blow!" Minella whispered anxiously, "Or it will be no use. And by the way, I can tell you, that even if you cut her head off it won't kill her, she has got another three lives. If you kill the witch, she will then become a cat, and if we manage to kill the cat, she will become a magpie, and if we also should manage to kill the magpie, she will finally escape us in the shape of a pike. So you see it is useless to try!"

Nothing, however, could prevent Tittone from carrying out his intentions. "I've come here to finish off that terrible witch,

and die she shall, however many lives she may have to gamble with," he retorted in a whisper.

Carefully he shut the door after them and went up to the bed. Pudullia lay there still snoring, terrible to behold, with her broad mouth wide open, puffing out snores, her beak-like nose sticking up in the air, and her claw-like fists clenched on the blanket.

Tittone drew his sword and with all his force he cut her head right off. Next minute a big black cat jumped down from the bed.

Minella and Tittone chased her about in the room, but the cat jumped up on chairs and tables, and finally made a spring up to the open window and jumped straight out.

Tittone and Minella rushed as fast as they could out into the garden. Just as they caught sight of the big black cat, it disappeared into some thick bushes. Then Tittone remembered his little silver box, and taking it out of his pocket he picked out the three hairs he once had got from the wild boar. He threw them on the ground, stamped on them and called out, "This way! Brother Boar!"

At once a wild boar came running.

"Catch that big black cat under the bushes over there! It's Pudullia!" shouted both Minella and Tittone, pointing to the bushes.

Like lightning the wild boar set off. They saw him rustling under the bushes until a big black cat jumped right out on top of him and was instantly killed by his strong tusks. In the same moment the wild boar disappeared, and there stood Prince Rollo, as handsome as ever. He embraced his sister and shook hands with Tittone. In the excitement of seeing each other again they had almost forgotten Pudullia, who, in the shape of a magpie, was sitting in a high tree and with a scornful laugh made herself known.

"That's a magpie! Look at the magpie up there! It must be Pudullia!" cried Minella pointing to the tree. It was useless to think of climbing a tree to try and catch a bird. But Tittone took out the three feathers from his little box and let them fly up in the air. "This way! Brother Eagle!" he called out.

Instantly a large eagle came soaring over their heads.

"Kill the magpie up there in the tree! That's Pudullia!" all three of them shouted to the eagle.

The eagle pounced swiftly on the magpie and tore it to death with his strong talons. As soon as this happened the magpie disappeared—but so did the eagle. Prince Rillo, in his human shape, stood in front of Tittone and his brother and sister. They laughed and embraced each other in their happiness to be reunited.

"The pike! The pike!" Minella suddenly called out. "It must have jumped into the lake! I just heard it splashing in the water."

All of them rushed down to the bank of the little lake. There in the clear and shallow water they could see a large pike swimming about.

It took Tittone only a second to take out the three scales of the shark and rub them in his hand. "This way! Brother Shark!" he called out. The sharp fin of a big shark emerged at once from the water.

"That large pike out there, catch her! It's Pudullia!" they all shouted to him, pointing to the pike that was swimming hurriedly towards some beds of reeds hoping to escape there. But it was useless trying to escape the shark. It sped off like an arrow and caught her.

A valiant and handsome knight emerged from the water after a few seconds, holding a dead pike in his hand. It was

Rallo who had been restored to his human shape again the moment he killed the pike. The pike was Pudullia, and this really was the very end of her, for now she had not a single life left to use for an escape.

Now there was nothing that could disturb the rejoicing of the brothers and their sister. They did not know how to thank brave Tittone who had delivered them all from the terrible witch Pudullia. At last they felt it was time to leave Pudullia's gloomy castle and return to their own country.

Each of them took a fine horse from Pudullia's stable and they rode together through the wilderness from which they soon found a way out. Before long five tired but happy riders came to the Kingdom of Velprato.

The rumour had already reached the King and Queen of Velprato that their three sons and only daughter were on their way home, delivered from the witch by a valiant young Prince. But the unhappy King and Queen did not dare to believe it.

The Princess Fabiella, Vesta and Rita were at once sent for by their bridegrooms and the feasts and rejoicings that now followed were never forgotten by those who enjoyed them.

Tittone was, of course, the hero of the day, and the highlight of the celebrations was his wedding to Princess Minella.

Royal guests from fifteen kingdoms were invited and there was not a single one who did not come, for not even in those days was it common to have the chance of meeting Princes who had been turned into animals and back to humans again.

# Donkey-Skin
## A story from Russia


ONCE UPON A TIME there lived a King who was one of the mightiest rulers in the world. He was a terror to his enemies, but kind and gentle to his subjects. His palace was truly called the most magnificent in the world, for its splendour and richness were known everywhere. A multitude of courtiers and servants responded to his slightest wish. Beautiful flowers and rare trees flourished in his gardens.

In his stables were a string of the finest horses one could ever see wearing costly bridles and saddles embroidered with gold and silver. Surprisingly, the finest stall was given to a long-eared donkey. But this donkey had the extraordinary power of leaving a heap of golden coins on the polished floor every morning instead of droppings.

You may think it was all these things that made people call this King the happiest man in the world, but in fact it was something else. For the King was married to a noble and beautiful woman who was gentle and wise and loved her husband very dearly. When she bore him a little daughter there was no end to their happiness. And the Princess grew more like her mother each day.

Even the mightiest king can suffer bad luck and sorrow, and one day the Queen fell ill suddenly. A host of doctors and famous scientists were called to the royal palace, but nobody was able to cure the terrible disease that was killing her.

The King sat by the side of his beloved wife, and swore he would never marry again. He could not possibly find another woman as mild and good and beautiful as she was.

The Queen smiled at him and said, "My dear, dear husband and King, of course you shall marry again, but you must promise me never to marry a woman less beautiful, less good, and less wise than I have been.

"You may rest assured," cried the King, "It will be quite impossible to find another like you even if I looked for her round the whole world."

That was what the Queen wanted to hear, and she died contentedly in the arms of the King. The King sobbed in grief with his tears running over his cheeks.

After the Queen's death the King was inconsolable. For a whole week he shut himself up in his rooms and refused to see anyone. When at last he left his room and turned to his duties as ruler of a mighty kingdom, his beautiful daughter came towards him and flinging her arms round his neck she sobbed out her grief for she too had suffered a great loss. She no longer had a dear and loving mother. When the King looked up at her, for the first time he noticed that she was the very image of her mother, and his grief was greater than ever. From that day he could not bear to see his own daughter. But as he wanted to hide his feelings from her, he decided to give her to the first suitable man who asked for her hand in marriage.

Now it happened that a neighbouring King, an evil-looking old widower, as mean and cruel as he was ugly, came to ask to marry the young Princess. And her father, the King, willingly gave his assent.

The young Princess had heard many dreadful stories about the old King, who was said to have tormented his first two wives to death. So she went to her father and pleaded with him not to make her marry this evil King. Her father told her that he had already given his assent to the marriage, and a king must keep his word. Nothing could now alter the wedding although he would gladly fulfil any other wish she had.

The poor Princess went away deeply distressed. Who would now help her, when her mother no longer could? At last she remembered that she had a kind godmother with magic powers and she set out to find her.

When at last she found her godmother's house, she was surprised to hear her say, "Little Princess, I know why you have come here, and I know that your heart is full of grief. Here with me you can feel happy and safe, and perhaps together we can try to find some way of saving you from this hateful marriage. You can at least put it off for a while, by asking your father to grant you a wish he cannot possibly achieve."

When the King told his daughter that the day for her marriage had now been settled, the Princess said that if her father ever wanted her to be happy again, he must give her a dress as light and delicate as the sky itself, shining with glittering stars.

The sight of his daughter was so painful that the King felt he would do anything to make sure that she married and went far away. So he ordered the best dressmaker in his kingdom to make a dress for her as light as the sky, and adorned with glittering stars. He didn't care how costly it was, but he insisted it must be ready in four days.

There is no limit to what money and power can achieve. On the appointed day a dress was ready as light as the sky, embroidered with shiny stars of the finest silver thread. Both the King and the Princess had to admit that the dressmakers had succeeded in their difficult task.

The poor Princess did not know how she could avoid keeping her promise and marrying that hateful old King. She rushed to her godmother in desperation.

"Try once more," her godmother said, "Ask your father to give you a dress that is even more unusual, a dress so wonderful that even the bright and shiny stars will be overshadowed, a dress like the moon."

Again the King called his skilful dressmakers and gave them all the precious material they needed. After another four days they put a gown before the King that surpassed anything he had ever seen before, in palest pink colour with rays of glittering silver. The Princess had to admire this dress however sorry she was that the dressmakers had again been successful. But her godmother had taught her what to say, so she still had another wish.

"I would like a dress as radiant as the sun itself," she said. And the King had no choice but to call the brilliant dressmakers again and also his finest goldsmiths. This dress which should be more radiant than the sun itself had to be of costly yellow material embroidered with diamonds and pearls as well as gold.

Again the dressmakers created a masterpiece. The Princess turned sadly away from the wonderful dress, and to her surprise saw her godmother standing by her side, invisible to everybody but herself.

"You must ask for something so valuable that your father at last has to give up the whole wedding," she whispered. "Ask for the skin of the precious donkey in your father's stable; he will never be prepared to sacrifice anything as costly as that."

The Princess did as her godmother told her. The King, who avoided looking at his daughter, now looked her straight in the face reproachfully, but again he was overwhelmed by the same terrible feeling, so that he had to give in even to this mad and meaningless wish.

"But," he said, "this is the very last wish of yours I am prepared to fulfil. Your bridegroom has been waiting long enough for the wedding, and it must take place four days from now."

The marvellous magic donkey was killed and the skin was brought to the Princess. She thought this was the end and there could be no possible escape. But her kind godmother stood by her side, and told her how to escape.

"I will put your beautiful dresses and your precious jewels in a box, while you wrap yourself up in the donkey-skin. You also blacken your face and feet to make yourself unrecognisable. Then you can certainly feel safe, because no one would ever imagine that this ugly garment hides so lovely and beautiful a creature."

She also handed her a little golden key, and told her to take good care of it. "As long as you carry this key the magic box with your belongings follows you under the earth, wherever you go, and when you settle down anywhere the box will stand beside you." For safety the godmother put the key into a little leather purse, which she fastened to the inside of the donkey-skin.

Early next morning the poor Princess left her father's palace in her disguise. Everybody was busy preparing for the wedding celebrations when they suddenly discovered that the Princess had disappeared, just as the evil old bridegroom arrived with his whole retinue of courtiers and servants. Everybody in the palace had been busy, each in their special way. Some decorated the palace in the most fantastic way, others laid the tables with costly dishes, and in the kitchen the most delicious food was being prepared. And the ladies of the court were just putting a finishing touch to their headdresses adorned with glittering diadems.

When they discovered that the bride was gone, the commotion was terrible. The King sent people out in all directions to look for her, but in vain. The wedding could not take place.

The Princess, ugly and dirty in her new disguise, walked on without being recognised by anybody. The whole day she kept on walking and whenever she came to a large house, she asked if there was some work for her to do, so that she could earn her food and a place to stay for the night. Most people shuddered at the mere thought of having someone so ugly and dirty in their homes, but a few kind people felt sorry for this disgusting creature, and gave her some food and a barn or a shed where she could sleep.

She walked for days and days in this way, and many nights she had to sleep in the open air. She had left her father's kingdom far behind and when she came to a large house, she decided to go up to it. She stopped at the back door, and as usual she asked for a job to do.

"Well, we may just need a dirty thing like you," said the man who opened the door. "You can look after the pigs, and bring them their food, and there will always be some rags to wash up. We will certainly be able to keep you busy with one thing or another." He was not too unkind to her and showed her to the kitchen where she could get some food.

She entered the kitchen where all the servants were gathered, but their eyes rested on her in horror. They made her sit in a

dark corner, as far from them as possible. They amused themselves by calling her all kinds of names, and teased and scorned
her. When they asked her what her name was she only shook
her head in silence.

"Are you dumb, Donkey-Skin?" they called out to her.

"Donkey-Skin, Donkey-Skin. That's a good hame for her!"
they cried. But all the time the Princess sat quietly in the corner,
eating what was put before her. From now on her name was
Donkey-Skin, and she tried not to care about the mocking and
laughing around her. When she had finished eating, the man
who had given her the job took her along past the stable and
well-kept cowshed to the pigsty. He talked to her about her
duties, as he took her along a path through a field. At the end

of this path they came to a door opening into a tiny shed. Inside there were only bare walls and boards covered with straw, and in a corner there stood a small fire and a bucket for fetching water.

"You cannot expect to sleep in the house with the other servants," the man told her, "this will be your place. But before you go to sleep you must feed the pigs."

That night when she came into her little hut and closed the door behind her, she saw to her great surprise the magic box standing there beside her straw-bed. Tired though she was, she pulled out her little key and opened the box. Her kind god-mother had put a large velvet cover over her fine dresses. She had added a large mirror, comb and brush in silver and put at the bottom her jewel-caskets on soft fine cushions. The whole box was lined with fine tapestry.

She took out the tapestry and spread it over the floor and round the walls. She put the soft cushions on the straw-bed,

and covered them with the warm velvet cover. She placed the magic box beside her bed with the large mirror and her brush and comb on top. Now she had a dressing-table as fine as any Princess could wish for, and her miserable little shed had become quite a beautiful little room. The Princess took off her donkey-skin, combed her wonderful soft golden hair which had been hidden for days under the ugly donkey mane, and washed off all the dirt. Now she was so tired that she threw herself on her bed, pulled the velvet cover over her and fell asleep.

Her days were now filled with hard and dirty work, but her little room was a secret comfort to her, and even the servants' scornful remarks could not hurt her very much.

On Sunday mornings after doing her morning duties, Donkey-Skin had a few hours to herself, so she went to her little room, shutting the door carefully. She took off her donkey-skin, combed her beautiful hair and put on one of her wonderful dresses. Then she opened her jewel-caskets and made herself as beautiful as she could with her costly jewels. She was indeed a dazzling sight, and when she saw herself in the mirror she felt once more like the Princess she actually was.

She loved looking fine and clean again, and every Sunday morning when she had some free time she opened her wonderful box and enjoyed its contents. As soon as she left her room, she became Donkey-Skin once again, a laughing-stock and a target for everybody's mockery.

The owner of the house where Donkey-Skin now lived was a rich nobleman with a grand park, famous for its rare and wonderful animals. He was especially interested in birds of bright and unusual colours, and over the years had gathered all the remarkable birds he could find. There were peacocks, pheasants, and parrots, small birds like canaries, goldfinches and the smallest of them all—the little brightly coloured hummingbird. Altogether he had ten large houses of glass where he kept his birds.

The King's son had heard of this and decided he must see these wonderful birds. One day there came a message from the royal court that the Prince would be pleased to look round the famous bird-houses. The nobleman, very happy and honoured, invited the Prince to come to his estate and stay for some days as his guest.

The servants could not speak of anything else for the next few days: how noble and good-looking the Prince was, and what a fine sportsman. They discussed the food they were going to serve, who was going to brush his hunting-suit, and there was quite a row about who would have the honour of cleaning his boots. Even the dull and uninteresting Donkey-Skin could not help listening.

"What on earth are you standing about for, Donkey-Skin?" they cried to her. "You won't have the slightest chance of getting near our noble Prince. He would be scared to death at the mere sight of an ugly creature like you. Get back to your work."

The Prince arrived and the next day, when Donkey-Skin was fetching the food for the pigs, she was able to catch a glimpse of him. And even she, who had seen so many noble men at her father's court, had to admit that this gallant-looking Prince was unusually noble and handsome. This was indeed a Prince after her own heart, she thought. After all, she was a Princess, and this Prince could easily have been her bridegroom instead of the evil old King her father wanted her to marry.

Next morning happened to be a Sunday but the Prince expressed his wish to see the cattle on the estate. He went through the fine cowshed and saw also the pigs that had just been fed, then he walked along the path and discovered the door at the end of it. Longing to find out what animal was inside, he tried the door but found it locked. Full of curiosity he peeped in through the keyhole.

To his astonishment he saw a pretty little room and in front of a mirror stood a creature more beautiful than anything he had seen before in his life. Was it a fairy? or a goddess? this dainty girl with hair like golden silk round her gentle face, and in a dress more radiant than the sun itself, embroidered with gold and jewels.

His first thought was to break open the door and rush into the room, but there was something about her that made him hesitate, and so he returned to his host. He asked him who it was who dwelt behind that door at the end of the path, "was it a fairy or a human being?" But his host only shook his head, and said he didn't know of anybody. He called a servant and asked him if he could tell him who lived there.

"Surely, my Lord," he said, "you don't mean that ugly, dirty Donkey-Skin who looks after the pigs? She is so dirty that she is loathed by everybody, and hardly speaks to anyone. That's the only one I know of."

After another few days the Prince had to return home, without discovering who the mysterious Beauty behind the closed door in the pathway was. "Was she real, or was it only a vision?" From that day the Prince could not get her out of his mind. He was depressed, had no appetite and his health declined. The King became worried, and the Queen wept when she saw her dear son looking a mere shadow of his former self.

"What is it you want? Is there anything you lack?" He refused to eat, and his good mother didn't know what to put before him. "Surely there must be something we can cook to give you an appetite?" she asked him.

"Well, perhaps there is just one thing I should like to eat," he answered. "A cake made by Donkey-Skin, a maid at the nobleman's estate with the fine bird-houses."

The Queen found this a funny name even for a simple servant but if her son wished to eat a cake made by this person, he should get it.

She sent a message to the estate where Donkey-Skin worked and the messenger was told that Donkey-Skin was a girl, loathsome, black and dirty like a pig, and detested by everybody. "That won't deter me from insisting that she carries out the Prince's wish," he answered, for he knew that the Queen would go through fire and water to cure her beloved son.

So Donkey-Skin was given the order to make a cake for the Prince, and she enjoyed doing this, more than she had enjoyed anything that she had ever done before in her life.

She went to her little chamber, took off the donkey-skin, washed her face and hands carefully, combed her long fair curls, and put on her star-dress, so she was quite clean when she started making the cake. She took the finest flour, fresh eggs, and the best butter and honey, and stirred it all into a fine dough. But while she was kneading the dough a little ring dropped from her finger right into the middle so she couldn't find it. Dreading it must have rolled into a corner, she put the cake into the oven and as soon as it was ready she put on her donkey-skin again, and took it to the King's palace.

As soon as the Prince tasted the cake, he thought it was the most delicious one he had ever eaten. For the first time for weeks he suddenly developed a keen appetite and swallowed one piece after the other of the wonderful cake. Munching away he bit on something hard. Just in time he stopped swallowing and discovered a small, fine ring.

Now all his interest in the cake was gone, and all his attention concentrated on the little ring. It could not possibly belong to anyone but a noble Princess with fine slender fingers.

He carried the ring with him in his pocket wherever he went, and at night he put it under his pillow to dream of his goddess, his fairy or whatever she could be. But at least now he had evidence that she was real and not a mere vision which in moments of doubt he sometimes had feared.

After some time the Prince's health again began to decline and this time he seemed even worse. Again no doctor was able to cure him. Full of despair the King and Queen asked him if there was anything he wished that they could help him to fulfil. If he wanted to marry he could choose anyone, even if she wasn't a Princess or a noble lady, if it would only make him well again. The Prince was now so weak that he had to stay in bed.

"Yes," said the Prince, "I really do want a bride, but I shall only marry the person that this ring fits, whoever she may be," and saying this he took the precious little ring out from under his pillow and held it out to his astonished parents. They did not dare contradict him in his present state of health.

The King sent out his heralds with trumpets and drums to announce that anyone, whoever they may be, should come to the palace and try on a ring, and the one it fitted was to marry the Prince.

The first to make the test were all Princesses, countesses and noble ladies, but when they tried the ring it would not fit any of them. Round about the country, fine ladies and young girls did everything they could to make their fingers thinner, but in vain. They all came to the palace where the Prince, who had recovered a little, sat trying the ring on every finger. Now came the less noble girls with the farmer's daughters and servants. Finally the King and Queen thought that there could not be a single girl in the whole country who hadn't tried the ring on her finger, and the herald announced that the test was over and there wasn't one finger that fitted into the ring.

The Prince then called out in desperation, "Is there really no one left who has not tried the ring on her finger?"

"Well of course there is dirty Donkey-Skin," cried a scullery maid scornfully, "but she isn't fit to come in here!"

"Why not?" interrupted the Prince.

"Well, how could a disgusting creature like her be allowed into the presence of the Prince? Anyway it's obvious the ring would never fit on her filthy fingers."

"Let her come in!" was the Prince's order.

When Donkey-Skin came, she stretched out a little fine white hand with rosy nails from the dark dirty donkey-skin towards the Prince, and he slipped the ring on her slender finger where it fitted exactly. Everyone was amazed, and murmured in wonder.

Now the court advisers wanted to bring Donkey-Skin before the King at once. But she begged to be allowed to wash and change her dress to make herself a little more presentable to see the King.

After a little while a lovely lady entered the room in the palace. Her silvery gown was radiant like the moon, her golden soft hair lay in long curls round her pretty face, and with her slender figure and elegant bearing she looked indeed a Queen.

And the Prince at once recognised the fairy of his dreams, whom he had only seen once through the key-hole. He threw himself at her feet and asked her to marry him. Then he took her to his parents and presented his bride to them. They were enraptured by her beauty, and asked her to tell them her story.

And now a second wedding party was arranged for the Princess. This time more happily. Invitations were sent out to many royal courts including the Princess's father. He had felt sad and guilty after she had run away, and was overjoyed to see her at the side of a young and noble prince. And the Prince, who would have been satisfied to marry his beautiful bride, even if she had been only a poor little servant, was still pleased to find that she was the daughter of a mighty King.

The fairy godmother was an important guest at the wedding for the Princess owed her so much; for without her help, she would never have survived her days of distress.

# Sampo-Lappelill
## A story from Lapland, by Z. Topelius

ONCE UPON A TIME there was a Lapp-man and a Lapp-woman. Do you know what that means?

The Laplanders are a people who live in the north of Norway, Sweden and Finland, in the most extreme parts of Scandinavia. There you will find no fields or forests or houses, for their country is a strange one. One half of the year it is almost always daylight, so that the sun never sets in the middle of the summer, and the other half of the year it is almost always dark, so that the stars shine even in the middle of the day in winter-time.

For ten months of the year it is winter when you can go sleighing across the wide snow-fields in little boats which they call *pulka*. There are no horses to put in the shafts, only reindeer. Have you ever seen a reindeer? They are the size of a very small grey horse, with high branched horns and bright large eyes, and when they run, they go like a whirlwind up hill and down dale, so that their small hoofs go crack, crack on the ground. The Lapp-man likes to hear this when he sits in his pulka, and he wishes it could be like this all the year round.

This particular Lapp-man and Lapp-woman lived high up in Lapland at a place called Aimio which is near the River Tenijoki, or Tana. Here it is nothing but wild, desolate country. But the Lapp-man and his wife believed that nowhere on the whole earth could you find the snow so white and the stars so bright and the northern lights so splendid as those at Aimio. They had built themselves a hut there, in the way people usually do in their country. Trees do not grow in these regions, only very small birches, more like bushes than trees. There was nowhere they could get the timber to build themselves a proper hut, so they took thin, high sticks, and pushed them down into the deep snow, to form a circle, and tied the tops together. Then they hung reindeer-fells over the sticks, so that it all looked like a huge, grey sugar-loaf. And then their little hut was ready. But at the peak of the sugar-loaf they left a hole through which the smoke could escape when they made a fire in the hut. There was also a hole near the ground at the south side where they could crawl in and out. This was what the Laplander's hut or tent looked like. And the Laplanders thought it warm and comfortable, and got on splendidly in it, though they had no real bed or any floor other than the white snow.

The Lapp-man and his wife had a little boy whose name was Sampo, and that means "fortune" in Lapland. But Sampo was so rich that he had two names, one wasn't enough for him. Two strange gentlemen in big fur coats had once come and rested in their hut. They brought some hard lumps of white snow which the Lapp-wife had never seen before, and they called it "sugar". They gave a few lumps of this hard, sweet snow to Sampo and patted him on his head saying, "Lappelill, Lappelill!" (That is Swedish and means "little Lapp".) They could not say anything else as none of them could speak

Lappish. But the Lapp-wife liked the strangers and their sweet hard snow, and so she began to call her little boy "Lappelill".

"I think Sampo is a much better name," said the man angrily. "Sampo means fortune, Mother, and you be careful you don't spoil that name! Our Sampo will become the King of the Laplanders and rule over a thousand reindeer and fifty Lapp-huts. You just wait and see, Mother, you wait and see!"

"Yes, dear, but Lappelill sounds so sweet," said the wife. And so she called him Lappelill, and her husband called him Sampo. Now the boy was not yet christened, because in those days there was no clergyman within a hundred miles. "Next year we shall go to the vicar and have the boy christened," the man often said. But the following year there was something more important to do, and so they had to leave the journey for another year, and the boy remained unchristened.

Sampo-Lappelill grew into a plump little boy; about seven or eight years old. He had black hair, brown eyes, a snub-nose and a wide mouth exactly like his father, and in Lapland these features were considered signs of beauty. Sampo was not a delicate fellow for his age. He had his own small skis on which he swooped down the high ridges on the banks of the River Tana and his own reindeer that he put to his own pulka. You should have seen how the snow whirled about him when he slid out on the ice through the deep snow, so that only a tuft of his black hair could be seen.

"I can never feel safe until the boy is christened," said the Lapp-wife. "One day the wolves may take him out there on the mountain. Or he may come across Hiisi's own reindeer with the golden horns. And God bless the poor wretch who isn't christened then!"

Sampo happened to overhear these words, and began to ponder over a reindeer that was so magnificent it had golden horns.

"That must be a splendid reindeer, Mother," he said. "I should like to harness him to my pulka and drive to Rastekais with him!" Rastekais is a very high and desolate mountain which can be seen from forty or fifty miles away, even from Aimio.

"Don't you dare to talk such nonsense, you reckless boy!" scolded his mother. "Rastekais is the home of the trolls, and that is where Hiisi himself lives."

"Hiisi, who is that?" asked Sampo. His mother was confused. "What ears that boy has got!" she thought. "I should be more careful what I say. Still, never mind, he may as well be warned now about Rastekais."

And so she said, "My dear Lappelill, please never, never, go to Rastekais. There lives Hiisi, the huge, wicked mountain troll, king of all the trolls in the mountains. He eats a reindeer in one gulp, and swallows little boys as if they were gnats!" At these words Sampo looked very thoughtful, but did not say anything aloud. Secretly, he whispered to himself,

"It really would be something *extraordinary* to see a giant like the Mountain King once—but of course, only at a great distance!"

It was three or four weeks after Christmas, and still it was quite dark in Lapland. There was no morning, afternoon or evening, only night, and the northern lights sparkled both night and day. Sampo found it rather monotonous. It was such a long time since he had seen the sun that he had almost forgotten what it looked like. And when someone spoke about summer, Sampo did not remember anything about it except for the terrible gnats which almost ate him up. So Sampo thought that the summer could just as well stay away altogether, except that it would be light again, and he could see his way better when he went skiing.

One day at noon, although it was still dark, the Lapp-man said, "Come here my son, and you will see something!"

Sampo crept out of the hut and looked away to the south where his father pointed. Then he saw a little red stripe far down on the horizon.

"Do you know what that is?" asked the Lapp-man.

"It must be the southern lights," said the boy, who knew perfectly well the four compass points and that you couldn't possibly see the northern lights in the south.

"No, dear, this is the first sign of the sun. Tomorrow, or the day after tomorrow, we may perhaps see the sun itself. Look there, how strangely the red light shines on the peak of Rastekais!"

Sampo turned westwards and saw how the snow looked red in the distance on the dark, grim peak of Rastekais that he hadn't seen for a long, long time. Suddenly he thought again how thrilling it would be to see the Mountain King. Sampo brooded on his idea all day, and half the night. He should have gone to sleep, but he couldn't.

"No," he thought, "it would be too *fantastic* to see the Mountain King even once." And after thinking this over and over again, he finally crept out from under the reindeer-fell where he was lying and through the opening of the hut. Outside it was so cold that the stars sparkled and the snow crunched under his feet. But Sampo-Lappelill was no faint-hearted fellow, and these things didn't bother him in the least. Besides, he had his skin-jacket, skin-coat, skin-hood, and his skin-mittens. Thus equipped, he stood looking at the stars wondering what to do next. Then he heard, not far away from where he stood, his little reindeer scratching in the snow.

"Well, what about a nice little ride?" thought Sampo. No

sooner said than done. Sampo put his reindeer into the shafts of his pulka, as he so often had done before, and slid off, whizzing across the immense snowfield.

"I'll ride towards Rastekais—but only a very little way," he thought to himself. And off he went across the frozen River Tana and up the other bank at full speed.

There is a song called *Run my Good Reindeer,* a favourite of all Swedish and Finnish children in those days. Sampo knew it well, though he had never seen the book where it was printed, in which there was a picture of a Lapp-boy riding in his pulka behind his reindeer. That might have been a picture of Sampo-Lappelill himself as he sat driving across the snow singing the song to himself,

> "Short is our day,
> Our road so long,
> Hurry to my song.
> Hasten, quick away!
> Do not halt, my dear,
> Only wolves live here."

And while Sampo was singing, he saw in the darkness the wolves like grey dogs around his pulka, snatching at his reindeer. But Sampo didn't care, because he knew that no wolf was as swift-footed as his own good reindeer. On he rushed, the wind tearing past his ears! Crack, went the sound of the hooves of his reindeer, and the moon ran a race with him, and the high mountains seemed to run backwards. Sampo was so thrilled nothing else mattered to him.

Suddenly, in a sharp turning downhill, Sampo was thrown out and landed in the deep snow. But his reindeer didn't notice anything. He thought Sampo was still sitting in his pulka and ran on as before. Sampo had his mouth full of snow and could not cry "ptrruh! ptrruh!" after him. There he lay, like a little mountain-rat in the middle of the vast snow desert where no man lived for almost fifty miles.

At first Sampo was a bit confused, which you may well understand. He tried to crawl up out of the deep snow, and discovered that he was not hurt at all. But that didn't help him much. For as far as he could see in the dim moonlight there was nothing but snowdrifts and high mountains all around him. But there was one mountain that loomed up high above all the others and Sampo realised that he was almost at Rastekais. With a flash he remembered that it was here that the cruel Mountain King lived, who ate reindeer in one gulp and swallowed little boys as if they were gnats. Then Sampo-Lappelill became frightened. Oh, how he wished he could be home again with his father and mother in their warm hut! But how could he get there? And supposing the Mountain King found him in the snow, and swallowed him up with trousers and mittens like another little gnat-wretch?

All alone Sampo sat in darkness, in deep snow in the midst of the desolate mountains of Lapland. And it was so eerie, and frightening to see in front of him the huge, black shadow of the mountain Rastekais where the Mountain King lived. It didn't help him at all to sit there crying, for all his tears froze into ice and rolled like peas down his shaggy reindeer-jacket. So, after a while Sampo cheered up, and jumping up from the snow, started to run to keep himself warm.

"If I stay here, I shall freeze to death," he said to himself. "Well then, I would rather go to the Mountain King. If he is going to eat me up, he eats me up. But I'll tell him that he would do better to eat the wolves here on the mountain. They have much fatter steaks than I have, and besides, he'll have less trouble with their fells."

After making this decision Sampo started climbing up the high mountain. He had not gone very far before he heard something pattering in the snow, and almost at once a big shaggy wolf appeared beside him. That gave Sampo's little Lapp-heart a jump, but he decided to pretend that he wasn't at all frightened.

"Don't run into me like that! Get out of my way!" he shouted to the wolf. "I've a message for the Mountain King, and mind your fell if you dare touch me!"

"Well, well, well, take it easy!" the wolf answered (for on Rastekais all animals can talk). "And by the way, who are you, little boy, ploughing through the snow?"

"I am Sampo-Lappelill," answered the boy, "but who are you?"

"I am the Chief of the Mountain King's many wolves," answered the beast. "And I've been running about in the mountains to gather his people to the great sun-feast. As you and I are going the same way, you may as well jump on my back and you can get a ride up the mountain."

Sampo didn't hesitate long. He jumped up on the shaggy back of the wolf who galloped off, leaping over clefts and rocks.

"The sun-feast, what does that mean?" asked Sampo.

"Don't you know?" said the wolf. "When it has been dark the whole long winter here in Lapland, and the sun rises in the sky again for the first time, we celebrate the occasion. All animals and all trolls in Scandinavia are called to a meeting on Rastekais, and that day no-one must do any harm to anyone else, whoever he may be. Good luck to you Sampo-Lappelill, for you may rest assured that otherwise I should have eaten you long ago."

"Does the Mountain King also obey the same rule?" asked Sampo.

"Oh yes, certainly," said the wolf. "For one hour before sunrise and one hour after sunset the Mountain King himself doesn't dare to touch a hair of your head. But just you look out! When the hour has come to an end, and you are still on the mountain, a hundred thousand wolves and a thousand bears will rush on you, and the Mountain King will seize the one who first gets hold of you and then it will be the end of Sampo-Lappelill."

"You might perhaps be so kind as to help me, if my life is in danger?" asked Sampo with his heart in his mouth.

The wolf began to laugh (for on Rastekais wolves can laugh). "Put that thought right our of your head, dear Sampo," he answered. "On the contrary, I shall be the first one to lay my paws upon you. You are a nice, well-nourished little fellow. You are going to taste wonderful for an early breakfast in the morning."

Sampo wondered if he hadn't better jump off at once from the back of the wolf. But it was too late. They had arrived at the peak of the mountain, and there they saw a strange and wonderful sight.

The Mountain King himself sat on his throne of rocks that reached high above the clouds, looking far out over mountains and valleys in the night. On his head he wore a hood of white snow-clouds, his eyes were like the full moon when it rises over the forest, his nose was like a mountain-peak and his mouth like a cleft in a rock. His beard was like a tuft of long icicles, his arms like the highest firs on the mountain, his hands like bundles of fir-branches, his legs and feet like the steepest tobogganing-slides in wintertime, and his white coat like a snow-mountain.

You may wonder how it was possible to see anything of the Mountain King and his people in the middle of the night. But you must imagine how the snow was shining bright all round, reflecting the brilliant northern lights high up in the sky, and lighting the whole mountain-world.

Round about the Mountain King there were millions of trolls, huge mountain-trolls, ordinary wood-trolls, and small dwarf-trolls, so grey and tiny that when they trod on the crust of the snow, the tracks of their feet were no bigger than those of a squirrel. They had gathered here from the utmost ends of the world, from Novaja Zemlja, Greenland, and Iceland, yes, even from the North Pole itself, to worship the sun in fear, hoping to keep safe from it. For the trolls hate and dread the sun and would rather it never rose again when it set behind the desolate mountains.

And behind the trolls there stood all the animals of Lapland, big and small, in dense rows, thousands and thousands of them, from the bears and wolves to the innocent reindeer and the small mountain-rat, and the quick little reindeer-flea. The tiny gnat couldn't appear and was excused because it would have caught its death of cold.

All this Sampo saw with great astonishment, but then he slipped down unobserved from the back of the Chief Wolf, and hid behind a big stone to see what would happen next.

The Mountain King lifted his high head, so that the snow spun around him. Now the northern lights shone brighter than ever before, so that they formed a glory round his forehead. They flickered out in long star-like, rose-coloured rays over the dark, night sky. They flashed and flared, now large, now small, sometimes bright, and sometimes fading out, so that one ray of light after another swept past over the snowy mountains. It was in this way that the Mountain King enjoyed himself.

Then he clapped his icy hands, to make thunder rumble among the echoes in the mountains. And the trolls squeaked for joy, and the animals roared in fear. But that amused the Mountain King still more, and he bellowed out loudly over the mountain world,

"Let the weather remain like this so that it shall be forever winter and forever night! This is how I like it!"

"Yes, yes, yes!" shouted the trolls at the top of their voices, because all of them preferred night and winter to summer and sunshine. But from the animals there came a great deal of grumbling, for although the beasts of prey and the mountain-rats liked the trolls, the reindeer and the rest of the animals liked the summer except for the gnats that came out and drove them mad. Only the little reindeer-flea wanted summer without any reservations, and so she shrieked at the top of her voice, "I thought we came here to wait for the sun?"

"Oh, shut up, you miserable wretch!" growled the icebear beside her. "It's only an old custom that brings us together here. But this year we shall rejoice, this year the sun will stay away for ever. The sun has burnt out! The sun is dead!"

"The sun has burnt out!" muttered all the animals, and a shiver of fear passed through them. But the trolls laughed so much that their hoods flew off. And the huge Mountain King opened his mouth again shouting in his thunderous voice over the desolate mountains,

"It shall stay like this forever! The sun is dead! The whole world shall fall down on their knees to worship me, the King of the eternal winter and the eternal night."

This was too much for Sampo-Lappelill where he sat behind the stone. He rose, and taking a step forward towards the King, shouted out, like the impertinent little sauce-box he was,

"You are telling a lie, Mountain King! You are telling the biggest lie of your life. Yesterday I saw the first sign of the sun in the sky, and it isn't dead. Your beard will still melt when midsummer draws near."

At these words the forehead of the Mountain King grew dark, like a black thundercloud, and forgetting the law he raised his terrible long arm, and tried to smash Sampo-Lappelill. But just then the northern light faded away, and a streak of red light spread across the sky, shining right in the middle of the Mountain King's frosty face, so that he became dazzled and let his arm fall. Then the golden edge of the sun slowly rose above the horizon, giving light to the mountain world, the snow drifts, the clefts, the trolls, the animals, and the stout little Sampo-Lappelill.

The snow shimmered as if a million roses had dropped softly onto it, and the sun shone straight into everybody's eyes and deep down into their hearts. Even those who had rejoiced at its death were now delighted to see it again. The funniest sight was the amazement of the trolls. They peered at the sun with their small grey eyes under their red hoods, and its splendour dominated them even against their will, so that they went tumbling head over heels in the snow. The beard of the terrible Mountain King started to melt, and dripped down his wide coat like a running brook.

But while they were all gazing at the sun, the first hour almost sped past. Sampo-Lappelill heard one of the reindeer saying to her little kid,

"Hurry, hurry, my dear child, we must away at once, or we will be eaten by the wolves!"

And then he remembered what would happen to him if he stayed any longer.

He looked round hurriedly, and seeing beside him a splendid reindeer with fine, golden horns, did not hesitate but jumped up on his back and set off galloping down the steep side of the mountain.

"What queer cracking noise is that behind us?" asked Sampo after a while, when he was able to draw breath again after the speedy ride.

"That comes from the thousand bears which are lumbering behind us to eat us up," said the reindeer. "But don't be afraid, I'm the Mountain King's own Magic Reindeer, and no bear has hitherto snapped my heels."

And they rode on for a while again. Then Sampo asked, "What queer panting is that behind us?"

The reindeer answered, "That comes from the hundred thousand wolves which are galloping after us to tear you and I into pieces. But don't be afraid, no wolf has yet been able to win a race with me in the mountain world."

They galloped away for a while again. Then Sampo asked,

"Can that be a thunderstorm in the mountains which we can hear behind us?"

"No," said the reindeer, shivering from head to toe, "it's the Mountain King, who is rushing with giant steps after us, and now it will be the end of us both for no one can escape him!"

"Isn't there any way out?" asked Sampo.

"Our only hope would be to reach the vicarage, over there, on the bank of Lake Enare. If we can only get there we are safe, for the Mountain King has no power over those who are christened."

"Yes," cried Sampo, "run my good reindeer, run as swiftly as the wind, and I shall give you golden oats to eat out of a silver crib!"

And the reindeer ran for dear life, but they had just reached

the vicarage when the Mountain King rushed into the yard and knocked at the door with such force that everyone thought that the whole house would fall into pieces.

"Who is there?" the vicar asked.

"I, the Mountain King," answered a thunderous voice. "Open to the Mountain King! You have an unchristened child, and all such children belong to me."

"Just wait a little till I get my clerical coat and bands. A mighty gentleman like you requires a worthy reception," answered the vicar from within.

"All right then," roared the Mountain King, "but hurry up or I'll smash the wall of the house!"

"At once, at once, Your Grace," answered the vicar.

But inside the house the vicar siezed a bowl of water and christened Sampo in the name of God the Father, the Son, and the Holy Ghost, so that he now became a Christian.

"Well, aren't you ready yet?" shouted the Mountain King, and lifted his enormous foot to destroy the whole house. At that moment the vicar himself opened the door and said, "Get you gone, you King of night and winter. You no longer have any power over this child, he belongs to the Kingdom of God."

At these words the Mountain King flew into a rage so terrible that he cracked into tiny pieces. Thousands of millions of snow-flakes whirled round the skies in a terrible blizzard. So thickly did the snow fall that it almost reached over the roof of the vicar's house. Everybody inside feared they would be buried under the heavy snow. Only the vicar was calm and said his prayers, waiting for dawn to come.

And when the morning came, the sun shone on the snow, and it melted away, and the vicarage was safe. But the Mountain King had disappeared, and nobody knows for certain where he has gone although some people believe that he is still alive and reigns over the mountain Rastekais.

Sampo-Lappelill thanked the good vicar and borrowed a pulka from him. Then Sampo put the reindeer with the golden horns in front of the vicar's pulka and drove home to his father and mother in Aimio. And there was great rejoicing when he returned home so unexpectedly.

But how Sampo later bacame a noble gentleman who fed his reindeer with golden oats out of a silver crib, is another story, too long to be told now. It is said that the Laplanders from that time no longer postpone the christening of their children from year to year as they used to. Who would like his child to be taken by the wicked Mountain King? Sampo-Lappelill knows what that means, and he also knows what has happened when he hears a thunder-storm rambling round the mountains.

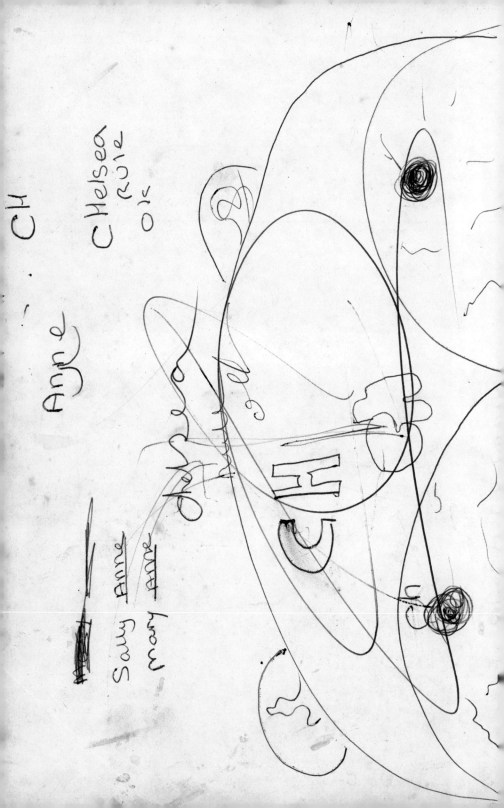